MW00814791

Also from Second Wind Publishing

by Charles Patton

Oriental Flyer

www.secondwindpublishing.com

Centaur of the Savannahs

By

Charles Patton

Savage Books
Published by Second Wind Publishing, LLC.
Kernersville

Savage Books
Second Wind Publishing, LLC
931-B South Main Street, Box 145
Kernersville, NC 27284

First Savage Books edition published December, 2014
Savage Books, Running Angel, and all production design are trademarks of Second Wind Publishing, used under license.

For information regarding bulk purchases of this book, digital purchase and special discounts, please contact the publisher at www.secondwindpublishing.com

Cover design by Stacy Castanedo
Photo by Mike Formy-Duval

Manufactured in the United States of America
ISBN 978-1-63066-077-0

Dedicated

To the many Formy-Duval family members who contributed to my knowledge of their family history, especially Mike Formy-Duval.

—Charles Patton

Winner of the
Clark Cox Historical Fiction Award
Under the title Crousilleau.

Preface

I have heard stories about Crusoe Island and the Formy-Duval legend ever since I moved to Lake Waccamaw, N.C. in 1984. What follows is fiction, based on a great deal of historical fact.

As I researched the story and tried to follow the family from France, I became aware of a remarkable and almost forgotten man and what happened in Saint-Domingue, now called Haiti, where the Formy-Duvals lived for about twelve years on the Crousilleau Plantation.

The man was Toussaint L'Ouverture whose actions greatly influenced Haiti and in all probability helped protect the southern United States from French invasion. The Formy-Duval's family story is tied to the Slave Revolt in Haiti and although they never met Toussaint, he and the Haitian Slave Revolt greatly influenced their lives.

Readers should not take this fictional novel as an accurate family account of the early Formy-Duval family history. Much of it is based on historical family accounts and family legend but much of it is also fiction.

Charles Patton
Lake Waccamaw, N.C.
March 2010

CONTENTS

Zoé
Dessalines' March South

Book Three – The Carolinas

Escape to the Sea
The Riverfront at Wilmington
The Waccamaw River
Crousilleau Island
Blood on the River

Epilogue

November 1, 1931
Baltimore Sun

A French Refugee Colony in Carolina

SWAMPS HAVE SHELTERED DESCENDANTS OF THOSE WHO ESCAPED HAITI MASSACRE

By Ben Dixon MacNeill

Thanks to the bear–hunting proclivities of the late Kinchen B. Council the outside world is beginning to hear of a hitherto unknown community in the swamp country of North Carolina. Twenty years ago, while pursuing a bear through the swamps of the Waccamaw river, in the southeastern part of the State, Mr. Council came upon old man Buck Clewis and a clue to a historical mystery that provided him with a hobby lasting until his death.

For the meeting with Buck Clewis enabled him to discover a remnant of French aristocrats who escaped the black wrath of revolting slaves in Haiti 127 years ago. Many books have been written of the unparalleled butchery during the Dessalines massacre in Haiti, which followed the French betrayal of Toussaint L'Ouverture.

Twenty years ago few people ventured into the wilderness that lay along the Waccamaw river as it idles through the swamps toward the sea after only the most casual effort at draining Lake Waccamaw...Seven miles

1

across the lake the swamp begins and runs, tropically remote, for forty miles toward the marshy shore of the Atlantic Ocean. The swamp almost touches the South Carolina line, but not quite. Here and there through the swamp, usually near the meandering river, lie wide expanses of hills that attain a relatively high elevation.

Twenty years ago it was a country to be avoided. It abounded in all sorts of wild game, especially bear and deer. But it also abounded in strange people with whom it was thought best to have little to do. They lived almost wholly in and by the swamps. People from the uplands dreaded any encounter with them; Negroes could not be driven through the swamps. The swamp people, so the stories ran, were likely to go berserk at the sight of a black man.

Since the beginning of the colony the Waccamaw swamp country was supposedly the receptacle of fugitives who could not maintain themselves decently in the established settlements. The swamp people were without schools or churches or any formal civilization. No good had ever gone into the colony, the people roundabout said, and no good ever came out of it.

Mr. Council was an inveterate bear hunter and he was possessed of an insatiable curiosity about people. He decided to venture into the swamp in pursuit of a bear. His family, of course, decried the venture and gave him up as hopeless. He was gone even longer than he had planned and when he came back he brought the skin of a vast bear and a face that glowed with a secret satisfaction. A member of the board of county commissioners, he surprised his confreres at the next meeting with the declaration that something in way of a school ought to be provided for the people of Cruesoe's Island.

Centaur of the Savannahs

Deep in the swamp, where his hounds were howling after the bear, Mr. Council had encountered Buck Clewis. Mr. Clewis was naturally surprised and taken aback, but in the face of a very genuine friendliness he overcame his obvious timidity and mistrust. There in the swamp a friendship was born that continued unflaggingly until... [Mr. Council's death].

It was probably a year-Mr. Council could not remember exactly-before the elusive intimacy between him and Buck Clewis was strong enough to foster a timid invitation for the hunter to come up to the swampman's house. The appearance of the house had something strange, a little incongruous, about it. To be sure, it was a rough thing of unhewn logs, but there was about it an echo of a grace, a shadowy charm that did not belong in the dim swamps. For a long time Mr. Council was not able to place it or to define it. Rather it was something felt, something sensed.

Later he discovered that the something he sensed had a clue in the contour of the stick-and-mud chimney, the sort of primitive chimney that chroniclers of the American pioneer have made familiar to everybody. But this chimney was different. There was an artistry about it. Instead of the raw sticks and mud narrowing into a flue, the sticks were completely hidden by a pinkish white plaster of native chalk and the lines of the chimney were molded into a smooth curve. The lip of the chimney was a smooth, chastely decorative line.

As far back as he could remember Mr. Council had seen stick-and-mud chimneys, but nowhere had he encountered one that was more than frankly utilitarian. This chimney was actually handsome. And that fact was filed away in his mind and taken home to be pondered over. The chimney just didn't fit into the pioneer, the primitive scheme of things. There must be something back of it.

It was a harassing winter for the bear in the swamps along the Waccamaw River. Mr. Council and the Clewises and the Sassers and the Duvals hunted them assiduously, and friendship grew between the swamp people and the toolmaker.

Swapping story for story with them. Mr. Council listened with growing fascination to the tales that the swamp people had to tell. And he wondered where they got the idea for decorating their chimneys. He feared that it would be considered rude to inquire directly about this and the mystery persisted until one day in his reading he came across a picture of a French country place. The chimneys in the picture looked vaguely familiar, and then there was no mystery about it at all. These chimneys on Cruesoe's Island were duplicates of the chimneys in the picture.

After that, bit by bit, as the islanders lost their furtive timidity with him and as he was able to turn inquiry deftly backward toward the beginnings of the settlement, the story began to piece itself together. Dimly remembered legends that had a singularly authentic ring of truth unfolded as he listened-and when he would come home he would set down the tale in fragmentary notes.

Some day he planned to get all of these notes together and set down the story of this fragment of French civilization that had escaped from the Dessalines massacre and had found its way to this remote swamp and taken root there. But somehow the quest was never quite complete; he was busy about so many other matters. First he must, over the opposition of his fellow-commissioners, do something for this newly discovered race. They must have roads. They must have a good school and a church.

Now they have their school and their roads and new

modern methods of farming and a church. In two decades the swamp has been transformed, transmuted. But Mr. Council died lately and the real story remains buried in the fragmentary notes that were twenty years in the making. Its verity has been checked as carefully as circumstances permitted.

The butchery of the French by the blacks in Haiti in 1804 [probably 1798] was not quite complete. Members of four or five families of rich planters somehow managed to escape to the coast of the blood-drenched island. There they found a small boat, scarcely big enough to hold a dozen people. More than twenty men and women and children crowded into it without provisions of any sort and shoved off into the sea.

Happily, it was the only boat in sight, and when the revengeful blacks rushed down to the shores in pursuit there was no boat at hand in which to follow them further. Later that day they were picked up by a bark headed for Wilmington, N.C. The master of the bark, when he discovered the identity of the castaways, was fearful. If the blacks set out to search the sea and the fugitives were found aboard his craft, things would fare badly with the master and crew. But there were women and children to be considered. He did not cast them adrift.

...He put in at the mouth of the Waccamaw river where it empties into the sea, thirty miles below Cape Fear, the entry into the port of Wilmington; and there he set the fugitives ashore, warning them never to disclose how they had come there. He suggested that they disappear in the swamp for the time being.

Making their way up the river, the band of refugees found the swamp not without inhabitants. Other fugitives, over past decades, had found refuge there. Nearly a hundred years before a band of Portuguese pirates, pursued by Spanish ships, had run their craft ashore near the mouth of the river, wrecking it. The Spanish landed and pursued them into the swamp. There they were, in the third generation, when the refugees from Haiti made their way into the swamp in 1804 [probably 1798-99].

...These were their neighbors when the group of Haitian refugees came to Cruesoe's Island. There they built a settlement and there they lived. An occasional wrecked ship off the coast brought them recruits and wreckage from which they made such necessaries as they must have. Sometimes there were arms and powder and sometimes tools and furniture.

Conditions were primitive in a degree that few colonies in the young republic had to endure. The fugitives from Haiti made themselves at home, hopeful that somehow a way back to France might be found. But they must have been broken in spirit by the sheer terror of what they had endured, and after a while the wilderness swallowed them. A new generation that knew nothing but the swamp and the plaintive, dull sorrow of the old women took their places. They became one with the people they found in the swamp, with the swamp itself. A century passed.

In this return to the primitive, these refugees gradually forgot the culture that should have been their inheritance. They forgot everything but the grim necessity of wresting a living from the swamp. Forgot even the spelling of their own names. Cluveires became Clewis and DeSaucerie became merely Sasser and Formy-Duval degenerated into a half-dozen unimpressive variations.

And gradually their speech degenerated. What must have been a pure French became something that was not French nor American nor Portuguese nor Spanish, but had some of the characteristics of all of them. Then, finally, American English came to occupy the dominant position. The fugitives brought with them a burden of terror that helped them to forget their native ways.

Even their legends took refuge in silence, except when the older people were sure of a friendly listener. Among themselves, handing them down from mother to child, there was the fierce hatred, born of terror, against black people, and the name of the island from which they had been driven was clothed with an especial terror. Someday, the legends said, a frightful vengeance would come upon the black people of Haiti, a terrible day of reckoning. This feeling is the most persistent of their beliefs.

It would be difficult to say-and Mr. Council was reluctant to hazard a guess-as to how many of the fifteen hundred people scattered over the occasional high ground ...of the swamp are descended from the remnant who escaped the black rebellion. Half of them, perhaps, would not be a bad guess.

There must have been some amalgamation of races and families in the remote isolation of the forest; but the French strain, even after a century and a quarter, is definitely apparent. It is predominant, if you stop to analyze individuals, to set them over against definite types of their neighbors.

Small mannerisms that belong to the French by inheritance, a kindling animation that does not belong to the Portuguese nor Anglo-Saxon nor American Indian.-nor to any combinations of these peoples: a swiftness to perceptions, a lithe grace of movement and of speech that flashes up through the reserve that more than a century of isolation has taught them; an instinctive hunger for something that is pretty-a characteristic that may be the survival of an inborn hunger for something that is beautiful.

"If you laugh at these young fellows I'll throw you in this river," Mr. Council threatened genially one Sunday morning, not long before his death, when we were approaching a small company of youths wandering indolently along the narrow road ahead of us. "Half of 'em, I'll bet you, have got strings of beads around their necks instead of neckties, but they like 'em, and you can like 'em, too."

With no shyness at all the youths –a dozen or more of them stopped-stopped to greet him. They were friendly and they were refreshingly eager about the prodigiousness of the automobile in which we were riding. Eight of them wore strings of gaily colored beads. It was part of their Sabbath raiment of festivity. They did not wear them with the solid solemnity with which a primitive man would wear beads; they wore them with a sort of insouciance, with a sort of gayety and their faces were young and eager and, somehow, very appealing. I liked the beads and the youths who wore them and I was not thrown in the river.

They were going to church. It was a primitive sort of service, under Methodist auspices. But Mr. Council had seen them, when he went to church with them, instinctively cross themselves when they knelt at the beginning to pray. Crossing themselves must be something that has come down to them through remote inheritance.

Two decades have passed since the modernization got under way. Housewifes along the lower Waccamaw are beginning to comprehend a little the meaning of a home demonstration agent and the uses of a community club at the schoolhouse. But they are still a little bewildered about it. Another generation, a generation that is growing up and away from the black canopy of fear that has shadowed the swamp, a generation that can look with indifferent tolerance upon an exceedingly minor and not at all menacing Haiti, is on the threshold of Cruesoe's Island, with its face toward a horizon with no brooding black cloud upon it..

A diminishing older generation still goes hunting for bear and talks in hushed, awed whispers of the legends of their grandparents and look wonderingly, not quite believingly, upon the younger generation that goes blithely about in automobiles, along roads that run straight where trails used to go windingly and which talks in a cadence that seems strange to old-timers.

One of this older generation is old man Buck Clewis. From the day when Mr. Council first went bear hunting along the lower Waccamaw to the day of his death he prized Clewis' friendship above that of many distinguished people. There was, there is, a peculiar something about the ancient bear hunter of the swamps. His dark eyes have a light in them that is at once defiant and pleading, at once bitter and soft, that is afraid and yet trusting, derisive and yet friendly. In him Mr. Council found unending delight.

To find Clewis's duplicate, outwardly, would not require much searching along the countrysides of France. His voice, softened in the mellow air of the swamps, is pitched high against the roof of his mouth, like a Frenchman's, and his syllables are clipped and precise, even when he is well along in the colossal tale of how he once inadvertently caught the largest bear that he ever saw.

It happened in the dusk of early nightfall, when Mr. Clewis was going along a shaded path in search of a sow that had wandered from her pen. She was a valuable sow and it would not do to allow her to wander alone in the woods. A bear might get her.

Presently Mr. Clewis saw her, ambling along, a dark shadow. In that day he was a very vigorous and agile man and he launched himself in a sort of a flying tackle, aiming to land on her back and divert her toward the pen. He would ride her home. But it was not the errant sow about whose neck Mr. Clewis locked his sinewy arms. It was quite the biggest bear he ever saw, and the ensuing ride has become an epic of the swamps.

There are still bear in the swamps, but they have retreated a little from the highway that cuts through to the sea and along which clatter the busses, hauling the children to the fine brick schoolhouse, where they all learn to read and to forget that a long time ago there were frightful things that happened.

First Printed November 1, 1931
Reprinted with the permission of the Baltimore Sun
Media Group. All Rights Reserved.

Book One

Formy-Duval

CRUSOE ISLAND

1816

They were coming again. It had been months since they had last appeared and it always meant the same thing. Someone was seriously ill down on Crusoe Island. It was a good thing they were coming out, because sure as hell, no one was going in there. They were mean, reclusive, and inclined to shoot first and ask questions later.

Crusoe Island was just a patch of high meadow, surrounded by the coastal swamps of southeastern North Carolina. They could have gone after another doctor in Whiteville, but their only exit out of the swamp was ten miles up the Waccamaw River and then four more miles across Lake Waccamaw to the nearest signs of any civilization outside of their own little world.

In the early 1800's a doctor was a rare commodity in the backwoods of the Carolinas; so they were coming after him, Dr. Ben Johnson, the only doctor in their region.

A trip up the river and across the lake meant there was a real need because it was not an easy trip in their little dugout boats. These were not like the canoes the Indians used, but had their own particular flair. They were made for narrow rivers and could float in only two or three inches of water. They reminded one of flat-bottomed European barges cut down to their small length and shape.

Most of their boats were made for one or two men but this one was big enough to carry three people and supplies which they occasionally bought from the outside world.

The two men in the boat had less than a half-mile to go when the doctor recognized their boat and odd hats. Even from this distance he knew they were coming for him.

"Elizabeth," the doctor shouted. "We've got Crusoe people coming across the lake; get them some coffee and biscuits while I get my coat and prepare my bag."

Elizabeth jumped up from her work and began preparing strong coffee and heating some biscuits left over from breakfast. She did not mind feeding these people from Crusoe but did have a strong fear-fascination about them based on the stories she had heard. These people lived a hard life in the swamp with only the barest of necessities. Anything they needed they built or grew themselves. They rarely came out and they tolerated almost no one in there, especially black people. It was said they would go berserk over the sight of a black person and if any law officials went in there, they were never seen again.

This reclusive atmosphere was just as well with the rest of the people in the county because there was nothing around Crusoe but snakes, alligators, and mosquitoes anyway. Those men who came for the doctor were small, wiry men but seemed to have the endurance of oxen. They would paddle ten miles upriver to get Ben, take him ten miles back to Crusoe, and then repeat the trip to take the doctor home. Ben said they never slacked their pace and didn't seem fatigued at all when they brought him back to the lake landing below his house.

They never talked much in Elizabeth's presence but

always thanked her for the special treat of coffee and biscuits in an almost genteel continental way with a slight bow of the head and quick phrases. One had even said mademoiselle once. She, like others, often wondered about their origin. It was 1816 and almost everyone's parents or grandparents were from Europe. Some thought the people of Crusoe originated from shipwrecked Portuguese sailors or maybe pirates forced into the swamps to flee an English government. Others said they were people who were outside the law and used it as a sanctuary.

Elizabeth couldn't quite put her finger on it, but these people were not like other English and Scottish immigrants common to southeastern North Carolina. Their whole demeanor was different.

Dr. Ben, as people affectionately called him, climbed down the steep lake bank and onto the small landing as the boat glided alongside it.

"We come to fetch ye, Dr. Ben," said the man in the back of the boat.

"I figured as much when I saw you on the lake," said Ben. "What's the problem?"

"We got a young'un cut real bad on his arm. We wus just going to bandage it tight and put 'bacca' juice on it but ole man Formy-Duval said to come fetch you."

Ben had heard about old man Formy-Duval before, but had never seen him in his trips there. They had only started using an outside doctor three years ago. He wasn't sure what they did for medical help before, but he suspected, strange as it might seem, someone had medical knowledge down there. He had seen two different incidents where someone had expertly sutured a calf muscle and had set a broken leg.

Ben had often thought about those two occurrences. No

13

other doctor was close enough to fetch or dared go in there. The only reason he was chosen was because the little village at Lake Waccamaw was the closest place with any civilization.

Occasionally they would come out to buy some supplies at the lake's small general store. Ben tried to talk to them and show kindness to them on the rare occasions when he met them. This was over a period of five or six years and he didn't think they knew he was a doctor until they appeared at his house one day, three years ago.

"You men come up to the house for some coffee and biscuits while I make sure I have extra sutures and cleansing lotion," Ben said.

The two men nodded their acceptance and tied the boat to the landing and climbed the bank. Ben knew from past experience that idle conversation was not successful with these people so he did not even attempt any on the walk up to the house. When the visitors reached the front yard, both stopped and froze in terror.

"What is it?" asked Ben.

They didn't answer, but Ben followed their gaze to the garden where two black slaves were hoeing. Ben had borrowed the slaves to help with the garden and a few other odd chores.

One of the men reached for the knife on his belt. "Whoa, Hold up!" Ben shouted. "What's the matter?"

"They's killers, black men will try to kill us," one of the men said.

"No they won't. These men are borrowed help and as gentle as any men I know. Holster that knife. I promise they won't hurt you."

The man holstered his knife, looked at his companion, and said something in what Ben thought was French.

"Come on in the house," Ben said in an effort to get them out of sight of the two slaves. *Maybe Elizabeth can calm them down*, Ben thought to himself. Elizabeth met them on the front porch with a tray of biscuits, jelly and mugs of coffee.

"Men, this is my wife Elizabeth. Sit on the porch and enjoy some of her grape jelly while I finish packing," Dr. Ben said. He did not bother to introduce the men because he didn't know their names. He knew they were wary about giving out information, particulary names.

Ben went inside and Elizabeth sat with the men. She was determined to have some type of conversation. They eyed her nervously as they drank their coffee; although they had on occasion talked to male outsiders, they had never before talked to an outside woman.

"I hope the coffee is not too strong for you," she said.

The men were surprised she actually spoke to them, but nodded their approval and continued with their rare treat of jelly. Anything with sugar was a treat. Although they had grapes on Crusoe Island, they did not have sugar.

Elizabeth thought she would ask a question that would force a response.

"Do you men have wives?" she ventured.

One of the men completely froze but the other one regained his composure and said, "Ah, we..."--long pause--"yes ma'am, both of us have women."

She first thought he was going to say, "Ah, oui madam," but he caught himself, and spoke what he thought would be acceptable.

"Are they from Crusoe or did you capture one of our fair maidens from around here?"

This rattled the men. "No madam, we would never take an outside lady against her wishes," one exclaimed.

15

"Oh, please forgive me. I didn't mean to accuse you; I was only joking with you," she said with a nervous laugh. She wondered if she had struck too close to home.

It took about thirty seconds but the men settled down to their coffee and biscuits and kept a wary eye on Elizabeth. Every now and then they cast a worried glance toward the garden.

The man who was doing the talking spoke and said, "John Paul's wife," nodding at his friend, "is from just across the swamp and my woman is from Crusoe."

Elizabeth sat back and thought about this last statement. Apparently some of them did go outside Crusoe Island for wives, although just barely. Everyone said they were all inbred.

The remainder of Elizabeth's time with the men was without any more conversation except when she excused herself and began to tend to her flowers on the front porch.

Ben came out with his medical bag. He had changed clothes to better accommodate a long boat trip and a brief walk through the high swamp meadows. Both visitors gulped down their last bit of biscuit and coffee, jumped to their feet, tipped their hats to Elizabeth as they passed her, and walked off with Dr. Ben. They held one hand on the hilt of their knives, and watched the two black men in the garden.

Elizabeth remembered the first time they had come after Ben. When he walked away with the men, she wondered if she would see him alive again. They were both in their forties and they had no children. He was all she had and Ben had never made any issue of no children. In fact, he had done everything he could do to convince her that he was happy with their lives. She was not ever fully convinced, but he was a kind and gentle husband and she loved him dearly.

"What are your names?" Ben asked, trying to divert their attention away from the garden.

It took a moment, but one of them said, "I'm John Paul and he's Michael."

"Well, how old is the young'un with the cut?

"Eight summers."

"How'd he get cut?"

"Plow blade."

"Is he running a fever?"

"Not bad."

It was always like that; only the shortest of answers, never anything extra.

At the landing, Ben let both men get into the boat, and then they steadied it by holding onto the landing. He stepped in carefully and settled himself on the middle seat as the men pushed off began paddling.

It was mid-October and the lake was flat and calm, so there was no trouble paddling across in the flat-bottom, narrow-sided boat. Had it been any other time of the year they would have come for him in a traditional Indian-styled canoe; V-hulled and high-sided.

Ben got comfortable, and slumped his head over for a nap. He knew this was going to be a three or four-hour ride and once he arrived in Crusoe not only would he attend to his primary patient with the cut arm, but he may have to tend to several people with an assortment of ailments. He also wanted to sleep during the crossing because once they reached the river mouth he didn't want to miss the beauty of the river as it meandered through the cypress swamp.

The gentle slapping of the paddles as they dipped into the water and the warmth of the sun on his face soon put him into a light sleep. Ben dozed for about forty-five minutes until the men began to back paddle, giving the boat

17

a braking motion. They maneuvered the boat into the mouth of the river.

For the next two hours Ben drank in the beauty of the small river as it snaked through the swamp. Cypress trees lined the banks and draped themselves over it like mothers holding umbrellas over their children's heads. The Spanish moss was thick in the trees and hung down like grey, grassy fingers from every branch. He never tired of this trip. It was a special beauty that reigned only in a few southern coastal states, and then only along a narrow buffer zone close to the coast.

Ben noticed Michael eyeing the trees closely as if trying to figure out something.

"What is it, Michael? What're you looking for?" Ben asked.

"Well, Dr. Ben, I'm looking for snakes; they'll drop out on you in a heartbeat if you're not careful," he replied with as serious a look as he could muster.

Ben knew Michael was trying to see if he could unnerve him, just for the fun of it. If it had been spring or summer time they would have all been watching the limbs but early fall just was not a high danger time for snakes.

Ben laughed at Michael's attempt to rattle him. He knew they could be pranksters once you got to know them, but he took one last look around for snakes, just in case, and decided that since they were in a playful mood that he might try talking a little more to them.

"Michael wasn't that you I saw in the store at the lake last year buying some mosquito netting," Ben asked?

"Ah, oui, t'was me Doc. Mr. Powell said I needed to buy some because they's so many skeeters in the swamp. I didn't think I needed it but he said it was healthful because skeeters carried sicknesses on'em. So, I bought some."

"Well, he's right," Ben said. "Some doctors on the continent say they carry the fever."

Ben let this sink in for a few seconds and asked, "Well, did it help with the mosquitoes?"

Michael quit paddling for a second and let the boat glide and then said, "Naw, I nailed it up between two trees and only catched two of'em." Ben didn't know whether to laugh out loud or try to smother the laugh with a cough, but then he caught Michael sneaking a look at him to see if he had swallowed his story and he knew he had been had.

Ben laughed and said, "You just keep paddling and mind the snakes." Ben could tell by the smile on Michael's face that he was pleased with himself by pulling Ben in on the story.

The rest of the trip down the river to Crusoe Island went by with only an occasional comment by Ben and an accompanying grunt or single syllable replies by Michael or John Paul. The conversation was sparse, it was nice to have nothing to do but take in the beauty of this dark cypress garden.

Ben never could tell how these men knew where to stop on this winding swampy river. There was something different around every bend but after a while it all ran together. All of a sudden, the boat glided up on the bank and there it was, Crusoe Island.

Michael pulled the boat on the bank while John Paul helped Dr. Ben with his medicine bag. Soon they were off on a two-minute hike to the few houses that made up their little community. Ben always marveled at how they found this high meadow in the swamp. What desperate measures would make someone seek out a place like this, completely surrounded by ten to fifteen miles of snaky, alligator-infested swamp with only occasional meadows of swamp grass?

Ben noted, that there must be fifteen to twenty crude wooden houses spread out for about five hundred yards; far enough to have some privacy but still close enough to holler if there was any trouble. The houses looked crude at first glance but on closer inspection they were well-put-together, and the chimneys always stood out in his mind because they were so different from the normal straight and non-esthetic chimneys of the English and Scotch settlements. These had a certain curvature and flair to them. Last year while visiting friends in Wilmington he had seen paintings of the French countryside with the same chimney shapes. How did they know how to design and build them?

Michael pointed to one of the houses and said, "That house." He put his hand up to his mouth and yelled out something toward the house. Ben couldn't quite understand it, but he followed him into the house.

The boy was lying in a bed in the middle of the main room. There was one older lady sitting on the bed mopping his forehead with a damp cloth and a younger one, probably his mother, talking to an old man in the corner in a dialect he could not understand, but probably French. The older lady made room for the doctor. Ben sat on the side of the bed and both ladies stood behind him where they could watch his inspection.

Dr. Ben spoke to the boy to see if he could establish some sort of bedside manner with the boy and maybe calm him in case he was scared.

"Hi there, I'm Dr. Ben. What's your name?"

"Henry," the boy said. He pronounced it *On-re.*

"Well son, how did you cut your arm?" Ben asked as he put his hand on the boy's forehead to check his fever. Any fever would give him an indication of the cut being infected.

20

The boy turned his head to the old man in the corner and waited. The old man gave a slight movement of the head to indicate that it was permissible to talk to the outsider.

"I was scuffling with Alexander and I fell on the plow blade." He paused a moment and then said, "Papa said he was going to whup us, but mon grandpapa said he had to wait until my arm got better."

"Well, let's take a look at that cut and we'll see what we can do," Ben said.

There was almost no fever so Ben knew somehow they had kept the infection to a minimum. It also meant that he probably did not have the fever that sometimes accompanied cuts on iron objects. *Thank goodness*, he thought, because it always meant a horrible death.

Ben untied the knot on the bandage and was startled to see the dressing had been finished with a surgeon's knot, not just any surgeon's knot either, but a type common for doctors in Europe. This was the third time he had seen ample evidence of medical training. He decided to ask about this after his treatment was over, when they had supper that night. He would have to spend the night and they would take him back in the morning.

The cut had a slight infection that was covered with an ointment that was having some effect. He hoped his cleansing and lotion would do as well as their local "poultice," as they called it. Their bandage was tight enough to keep the wound closed but loose enough to allow circulation. *Well done*, thought Ben.

"Now, son, this is going to hurt some when I start sewing to close the cut. Do you think you can take it?" Ben asked.

"I can take it. I'm like an Indian and Indians don't cry," his small voice croaked.

21

"Okay," Ben said. "Try to think of something else."

Ben pushed the needle through the skin for the first suture. The boy's arm jumped slightly and he let out a whimper but that was it; he didn't jump or cry anymore.

Suturing was one of Ben's specialties and a point of pride with him. One of his teachers in medical school taught Ben some special techniques the rest of the staff didn't think was important. Ben had noticed his teacher, trained in Europe, had patients with scars that were much less noticeable than other doctors, and over a period of time some of the minor scars disappeared. Ben had a reputation of being good with a needle and thread and not leaving ghastly scars.

Ben noticed the old man was standing over his shoulder, watching intently at Ben's suture pattern and the amount of pressure on each stitch. Ben knew this had to be old man Formy-Duval, leader of this tightly knit and secretive clan. The old man peered over Ben's shoulder until he finished closing the wound and began dressing it. Then the old man grunted what Ben thought to be an approval and went back to his corner and sat down.

The boy relaxed after his arm was dressed and soon dropped off to sleep. Ben turned to the two women and gave them instructions on how to use his cleansing lotion when they changed the dressing, which was to be at least once a day. The mother took keen interest and asked several questions and showed a good understanding of English, but Ben didn't think the elderly French-speaking woman understood a word he said or at best just bits of his instruction.

Ben went outside where Michael had a half a dozen people waiting for the doctor. There wasn't anything seriously wrong with any of them. One man needed to have a boil lanced, ointment applied and bandaged. Another had a cut on his hand that had never closed properly. Ben reopened it, stitched it, and applied some ointment. They all had small wounds and ailments, related to their hard work and a hard life.

Michael took Ben around the village after he had finished with his patients and showed him where they hewed out logs and made dugout boats; they called them "dug" boats. It took a great deal of skill and work to make these boats, but Ben soon learned that it also took a bit of practice to make the small boats stay upright in the water without tipping over. After inspecting the boats and taking a ride in a couple of them it was time for supper, Michael took him back to the house where he had treated the boy.

The boy had been moved to a loft and the bed had been pushed to a corner of the room. A table was in the middle of the room and was loaded with food. Formy-Duval stood up in the corner and indicated for all to take their seats. Everyone sat and then on some unseen command they mumbled some sort of prayer, crossed themselves in the Roman Catholic way, and helped themselves to the food. This was a good ole country meal with venison, sweet potatoes, greens, and freshly baked bread. Soon Ben's presence at the table became less noticeable. The conversation was sparse at first but increased after a few minutes. Ben listened to the problems of the deer and bear that plundered the vegetable gardens at night. Then the conversation turned to the safety of some of the more rambunctious children.

Henry's mother turned to Ben and asked, "Is there anything else I need to know? I want to know everything, because it's so difficult to get you here."

Ben thought for a few seconds and said, "Henry should be fine. Just keep changing his dressing and applying the cleansing lotion. If you run out of the lotion, use the poultice you have been using."

Ben paused a second and then led into the question he really wanted to ask, "If someone here can take the stitches out in about three weeks," Ben stopped, and watched the mother look at the old man and then nod yes to Ben, "then there should be no problem." Appealing to the group as a whole he said, "Apparently there is someone here who has some medical training. This is the third time I have seen where medical knowledge has been at work." Ben looked directly at the old man, "Would that be you Mr. Formy-Duval?"

The old man and Ben locked eyes and all went quiet around the table. Fear seemed to freeze everyone. It was as if a dark secret was about to escape. The old man finished chewing, wiped his mouth with a napkin and then spoke his first words, "Dr. Ben, you are most observant." The accent was what he thought was upper class French. Ben had studied French along with his Latin in college. "Indeed, I do have some medical training. I assisted French military surgeons when I was a young man. It doesn't take too many battles before you learn how to bandage properly or set a broken limb."

"But I have seen an excellent suture pattern when...", Ben managed to get out before he was cut off.

"The doctors taught me a few extra things to save themselves time during the rush of battle and dying men. They would stop bleeding, take out bullets, and I would close," the old man said.

"You either had a good teacher or much practice," Ben said.

"I was taught well and had too much practice," Formy-Duval replied.

24

The tension eased, and everyone continued eating. The conversation resumed but with a more guarded air. The rest of the evening went by without event. They sat on the porch for about an hour and Ben listened as the men talked about hunting, hunting skills, and other stories. When the evening social hour was over, Michael led Ben to his house where they provided a room with a bed, nothing else, just a bare room with a bed. It didn't matter to Ben; he was tired and was soon asleep.

The next morning after breakfast Formy-Duval walked Ben to the boat where two other men of the community were ready to paddle Ben back to his boat landing.

Ben stepped into the boat with his bag and a cured salt ham they had given him as payment. He watched the old man as they shoved off. On the spur of the moment and partly in jest he said, "*Au revoir*, Doctor Formy-Duval."

Formy-Duval did not let it rattle him and he took the statement for what it was, a friendly and humorous goodbye from a man whom he was letting take over his small practice because of his age and trembling hands. As they paddled away Formy-Duval sat on the bank and remembered when someone addressing him as doctor was a common and everyday greeting.

The last twenty years had been difficult years, very hard years, but at least they were alive. If they had stayed in France or Saint-Domingue, he, along with most of his compatriots, would have been dead. It didn't save his wife though, Jeanne Francois Duval. The change from being part of the royal court to a swamp princess, combined with four rapid childbirths was too much for her and she died soon after their arrival here.

Memories flooded his mind as he leaned against a tree and he allowed them to play in his mind's eye; something

25

he tried not to do too often. He let go of the strict control he usually maintained over his emotions, took a deep breath and let the old memories flow. They enveloped him in a flood of emotional snippets, each one a dramatic episode in his life.

1789

THE FRENCH REVOLUTION
"THE BEGINNINGS OF TERROR"

"DOCTOR FORMY-DUVAL, DOCTOR FORMY-DUVAL!"

Doctor Jean Jerome Prosper Formy-Duval stood looking out the window of his second floor garrison office, gazing at the port of LeHavre, France. More than a dozen ships were either docked, being tied to the wharf or casting off for foreign ports and continents. The afternoon breeze always brought the smell of the docks. Today it was quite pleasant. The ship below his window must have come from the tropics because his nose tingled with the smell of spices, coffee, and exotic unknown aromas.

The morning surgery had been tiring, and now after lunch with fellow surgeons and officers of the French army, he felt sleepy. He was almost in a trance and did not feel like moving his six foot-two inch frame from the window sill. The warm, summer afternoon breeze blew through his black locks of hair and fluttered the material on his loose, billowy shirt. He felt like taking it off and basking in the warmth of the sun, but decorum prevailed so he only had the top two buttons open. Below, street vendors were selling their wares to the sailors, soldiers were marching through the streets, and certain ladies with their parasols were trying to entice the sailors to go with them.

Somewhere in the back of his mind he knew this spell

was about to be broken. A small part of his mind was registering the fact that someone was running down the hall shouting his name. The rest of his mind and body was not about to move or break the trance until necessary.

"Doctor Formy-Duval," the young lieutenant exclaimed as he burst through the doorway, "the Citizens Committee...," gasping for breath, "they have arrested Victor, Romain, and Jacques!"

Jean snapped out of his trance and spun around to face his young friend, Lt. André Dubois. Jean heard what André said but he couldn't quite make his mind snap into action or even make sense of it.

"When?" Jean finally said.

"This morning, the Committee had four officers arrested here in LeHavre for being royalist sympathizers!"

"Where are they now?"

"They were put in the military garrison early this morning." André said, in a calmer voice.

"Damn!," Jean said. "Damn the Committee!"

Jean fell into his chair and thought about the fate of his friends. He could already imagine what had happened. His friends had been out at various taverns having their weekly contest, trying to determine which tavern had the best combination of ale, food, and friendly women. They did this weekly and made a big fanfare among themselves before awarding a decision to one of their favorite taverns. They had probably gotten careless and talked a little too loosely about their feelings for the present terror that was coming out of Paris and infecting the rest of the country. Someone had reported them to the Citizen's Committee. That was all it took to have one's death warrant signed. He was lucky he was not with them last night.

"When's the trial?" Jean asked.

"They had a special committee meeting this morning, and sentenced them to death tomorrow at ten o'clock in the morning." André said.

Just perfect for the big crowd of mid-morning shoppers, Jean thought and then asked, "Firing squad?"

"*Oui*, and my squad too." André said with a pained look.

"Your squad has execution duty tomorrow?" Jean said in disbelief.

"What are we to do, Jean? I don't think I can do it." André rubbed his hands along his cheeks.

"I can only imagine how you felt when the captain of the guard told you that your squad had the execution duty," Jean said.

"*Oui*, these are my friends. I have been on hunting trips with them; I have been out drinking with them, and even been invited into their homes. Now I am responsible for their execution."

Jean walked to the bookcase and leaned against it with his forearm against the books and his head resting on the forearm. For three years this madness had been going on around him and he had done virtually nothing to oppose it, but now it was touching his closest friends. Jean lifted his head, took a deep breath, and made a decision that would affect the rest of his life. "André, come to my house tonight after eleven o'clock. I think I have a plan," Jean said.

André slumped back in his chair. He knew whatever Jean was planning would probably end his military career and would put them on the run for their lives.

"Jean, what are you thinking about?" André said.

"I'm not sure yet, but when you come tonight be sure you are committed or don't come."

André knew the doctor would try to plan an escape for his friends. It was one of the reasons he was attracted to the doctor and his three friends, plain and simple loyalty. These men were as close to being brothers without having the same mother as he had ever seen. He was almost one of them. This would be his test, his initiation. Would he stand against this madness or would he fold and forever know that he had been presented the test and refused to participate?

André stood and walked to the door. When he reached the doorway, he turned, looked at the doctor, and managed to croak, "Tonight." He hoped he could live up to his word.

Jean watched as André left the room. He knew André was scared and had doubts about himself, but he felt he knew André better than André knew himself. He was certain the young lieutenant would join them. Jean had always been a good judge of character and chose his friends well. That was why he had allowed André to be part of their clique. He had seen class, dignity, and honesty in André and had initiated the invitations for him to join them on their nights out on the town. The other three protested at first, but if Jean insisted, then they all bowed to his wishes. Jean was the unproclaimed leader of this group. His quiet wisdom, quick humor, and friendly advice made him one of those few people whom everyone respected and wanted for a friend.

Dr. Formy-Duval spent the rest of the afternoon seeing his patients in the hospital and tried to do everything in a normal fashion. He did not want to do anything to arouse anyone's suspicions. Jean left the hospital thinking about his plan and how his wife, Jeanne, would react to what he was about to do and the implications for their family. He thought back to the night he had met Jeanne and the association he had with her family.

Jeanne Francois Formy-Duval had not always been so

strikingly beautiful. She always had potential, but during her pregnancy with their son Louis, her face and body had filled out to her present startling beauty. As a teenager she had become a five foot, seven inch, gangly goose with high cheek bones that gave her a gaunt look. Her height had made a loner out of her because she was taller than most girls and taller than half the boys she knew. Her hair was a dark auburn, which surrounded her face and complemented her green eyes. As a young woman, she had the appearance of a puzzle which was not quite yet put together. Boys would look and try to determine if she was pretty or not. Most of the time they gave up and decided not to pursue her any further because they had never seen anything quite like her.

Jeanne's grandparents were courtiers to the royal family in Poland and her father had been a military officer for the royal guard, thus they were heavily involved in the royal court affairs in France. Her sisters were eight and twelve years older than she and they had always been court favorites. Jeanne had been conceived when her parents weren't expecting it, and it showed in the way she was brought up. It was as if her family consisted of only the father, mother, and two older daughters who were constantly involved in the social affairs of the royal court. Jeanne was brought up by their maid, Henrietta, who loved her as her own and made sure from the start that she saw things from a realistic point of view instead of that foolishness of the royal court. Henrietta gave Jean a practical understanding of life. Jeanne loved her mother's and father's attention but learned not to fret when the family was gone for days and sometimes weeks at a time. Until she was seven years old she hardly received any more time or affection from her parents than a beloved house pet.

Her parents provided for her materially and made sure of the people they hired for the house lest someone mistreat their house or daughter. She did not suffer from her parents' neglect. Her emotional and loving needs were met by Henrietta and a house staff who pampered her. During the winter of her seventh year her parents were at home for a few months. They saw how she could be content with herself and did not need constant reassurance. Her desire to be a quiet and good girl and not ask foolish questions led her parents to the conclusion that she was not as smart as her sisters and might be an embarrassment in the royal court. The next spring she was in a nearby convent. The convent specialized in education for girls, and her parents hoped she would learn to overcome the appearance of dullness.

This setback for Jeanne could have been a crushing blow had it not been for Henrietta's skills at convincing her that this education process at the convent would be a wonderful adventure and opportunity. In fact, Henrietta felt this might be the chance to keep Jeanne from becoming like the other royal flits in her family. Henrietta visited Jeanne daily at the convent and was in constant conversation with her teachers about Jeanne's progress. One of Jeanne's teachers, Sister Yvette, became interested in her and became her mentor. Through the school's strong beliefs, good education, and strict ethics, Jeanne became well-founded in literature and the graces of the day. Her self-assurance, already strong, became unshakable. She didn't feel herself below or above any person and would look a person straight in the eye when conversing. Her development of class, self-assurance and the power of that direct stare unnerved people. It was not something she did consciously, but people definitely noticed.

The growth and procession of her education continued until she was eighteen. She went home that summer to be with her family. She was still tall, gangly and not all the pieces were together yet, but she was getting closer.

Her parents were having a party and it was supposed to be the big affair of the summer in their area, although toned down because of the political terror. Her mother and sisters had bought lavish clothes, wigs, and accessories for the party. They even bought clothes for Jeanne, but Jeanne had started shopping on her own. She found a seamstress shop that she had noticed as being able to fabricate unusual designs. It specialized in long flowing gowns, putting emphases on the body's natural lines. The seamstress used bold, solid colors with only an occasional tuck here and there. Jeanne and the owner had several sessions where they talked about the look she wanted to achieve. The result was a rich burgundy gown that emphasized her long waist line and a neckline that said, look at me. The seamstress showed Jeanne how to apply rouge to fill in her gaunt cheekbones and highlight other areas. She showed her how to apply coloring to emphasize the little cleft at the top of her lips and how to shadow underneath her lips with rouge to give them a puffy effect.

The night of the party she dressed late. She knew once again she would be considered unusual because of the simplicity of her dress and hair, but she knew it would be perfect for her. Jeanne put on her makeup and remembered the shop owner's words, "You have good facial features; don't use too much rouge; use it to emphasize; let it be as natural as possible."

Jeanne stood from the makeup table, took one last look in the mirror, smiled, and walked to the top of the stairs where the introductions were being made to the crowd. The head butler was making the announcements of arrivals when he turned and saw Jeanne. He gasped, not only at the beauty but at the audacity of the departure from fashion, the lack of frills and ruffles and a wig. He started to ask her if she had forgotten her wig but realized it would be a foolish question. Her whole appearance was self-contained and well blended. He smiled to himself. He knew this was going to cause a shock. He turned to the crowd and said, "Jeanne Francois Duval of Landerneau."

The statement, the elegance of the dress, and the beauty of her face stunned the party guests. The royal crowd was accustomed to seeing her two sisters and had forgotten that a third daughter was a contender for the royal clique. The room became silent; many people were confused because they had not realized that there was a third daughter. Envy swept the room because of the stunning effect she produced with her hair, dress, and beauty. Shock soon replaced envy because of the lack of traditional fashion, full of ruffles, lace, and wigs. The men were transfixed and many had their ribs lightly punched, or toes stepped on by their ladies.

Dr. Jean Formy had been talking with his friends when he noticed her approach the butler, but it wasn't until she turned to face the crowd while the butler announced her that Jean's mouth dropped open. Jeanne descended the stairs, grabbed the arm of her father and insisted he introduce her to all his friends. Her father could hardly believe this was his daughter. He blustered through a few words and took another hard look and decided this diamond was well worth showing off. He strutted around the room making introductions like a father with a newborn baby.

Across the room her two sisters could not move or take their eyes off her, but her mother, realizing the probable injustice to her youngest daughter, put her hand over her face and said, "Oh Jeanne, I'm so sorry." When she looked up, she saw Jeanne catch the eye of Henrietta, who was serving drinks, and blow her a kiss. She knew who Jeanne looked to for approval and love.

Jean was eventually introduced to Jeanne later that night but only briefly. Too many people were after her. He felt as if she had only acknowledged his presence among the dozens of other quests and surely did not even notice him. This was a girl he could take a serious interest in if she would give him the chance, but he doubted if he would ever get it.

Jean did not know it but he was a marked man. Jeanne had long heard about Jean from her sisters and had occasionally seen him. She had admired him for a long time, even to the point of having a crush on him. Jeanne made a point of staying at the party only long enough to make all the introductions and have a few polite conversations and then leave.

Jean was leaning on the stair railing as Jeanne started up to her bedroom. She stopped, took his hand, looked directly into Jean's eyes, made a daring decision to use his first name and said, "Jean, please come by the house sometime, I would love to hear about the school in Paris you attended and all your military adventures." She left her handkerchief tucked in the palm of his hand. Jean tried to say goodbye as she turned to walk up the stairs but he couldn't get it out.

The young doctor would soon learn that this was the way Jeanne was: direct, with a plan of action, and the courage to execute it.

Within a year Jeanne's plan was finalized when they married. They combined their last names to give them status, as was common in Europe. They became Dr. Jean and Jeanne Formy-Duval and because of the similarity of their first names, their friends started calling Jeanne, Princess, for her beauty and her family's connection to royalty.

The walk home from the hospital seemed to go by too fast. He dreaded telling Jeanne about his friend's fate and what he was planning. He could not get his mind to broach the subject with the right approach to tell her what was on his mind. Besides, it was hard to think about difficult things when it came to Jeanne. His mind kept crossing over to the more pleasant and carnal things about her, like the coy way she had of bending over in front of him wearing her night gown and almost completely exposing her breasts. She always pretended to catch herself and cover herself with her hand before she said, "Excuse me, cheri." But the recovery always seemed to be a little slow and was made with a tantalizing little smile.

Jean walked through the front door of their house and she was there to meet him.

"Evening, *cheri*," she said. "You look tired; want some wine?

"I would love some. Is Louis still up?"

"No, he was tired and I put him to bed a little while ago."

Jean took a sip of wine and watched Jean for a moment before telling her they had to talk. She must have read his mind because she turned and said, "I've already heard. Three military wives and two street vendors have already told me about the arrests."

"The street vendors seem to know everything first," Jean said.

"Yes, and they will be the ones enjoying it and screaming the most tomorrow," Jeanne said.

Jeanne had a wine bottle and two glasses on the table. She knew Jean would need to relax a little when he came home and she had designed it out as a way of sitting together and talking.

"What are you going to do?" she asked.

"You know I want to help them."

"What can you do without putting us in danger?"

"Anything I do will endanger us. It's just a matter of how skillfully I can plan it."

Jeanne put down her wine glass and gave Jean that direct stare and said, "I knew when I heard about the arrests you would feel that you would have to do something. I have thought about it all day, about what the consequences would be to you and me. I thought about discouraging you, but I don't think I could live with you or myself if we submitted meekly to their stupid little decision to end our friends' lives, so tell me, what can we do?"

Jean smiled at her. He should have known she would have already decided to help their friends. He revealed his plan to her and she helped him flesh it out. Over the evening they worked out a plan, or as well as a plan could be done with only a few hours of preparation. They decided on one more person to include. Jean's brother, Pierre. Jean did not really want to involve Pierre in this plan because of the possible repercussions. But Pierre was the only one Jean knew that had the sense of adventure, courage, and brains enough to help the plan succeed. Pierre, a bachelor, still lived on the family's country estate, a few miles outside of town. Jean had already sent a messenger to tell Pierre to come to his house as soon as possible.

André knocked on Jean's door at exactly eleven o'clock. The rest of the day and early evening had been mental torture comparing all the pros and cons of what he was about to get into. When it was time to leave for the doctor's house he wondered why he had tortured himself all day. He should have known that when the time came he was going to go, find out what Jean wanted him to do, and do it.

"Come in," Jeanne said, looking over André's shoulder to see if anyone was out in the street, "They're in the kitchen."

The word, "they" made André a little nervous. How many were there? Too many participants meant more chances of getting caught. He was relieved when he walked into the kitchen and saw only Jean, Jeanne, Pierre, and himself.

"Ah, André, you decided well, my young friend. Come, sit with us, and I will tell you what we're planning," Jean said.

Jeanne poured wine for everyone and Jean launched into his plan. "Gentlemen, tomorrow we are going to be illusionists. André, you are going to arrange for the muskets of your platoon to be loaded with gunpowder only, no musket balls. As the residing doctor I am to check the prisoners after the execution so I can verify their deaths. Tomorrow morning André and I will tell Victor, Romain, and Jacques about the plan. The problem is there is a fourth prisoner with them. I can only hope and pray he has enough presence of mind to play along with us.

"Now, look at these. Jeanne has sewn these small sections of pig intestine and will fill them with pig's blood. This small loop will be placed on the button on the inside of their shirts. When the muskets fire, our friends will fall down, faking death. I'll instruct them to fall in such a manner where they'll fall on the bladder of blood and break it. Then, I'll walk to them and verify their deaths.

"André, to make things look good, be with me when I

inspect the prisoners, and if something goes wrong and one of them twitches or makes signs of life, you may have to shoot at them. Just make sure you miss, but barely. If it's the fourth person, not one of our friends, and he can't handle the situation, then shoot him in the heart."

"Oh, Jean," André groaned. "This fourth person scares me. I hope he can act."

"So do I."

There was a short silence as everyone let what had been said sink in. Jean continued, "André, have your squad load the bodies as quickly as you can. Pierre, this is where you come in. I'll make sure the sergeant-at-arms knows you're there to collect the bodies. As soon as the bodies are loaded, take them to the edge of town where Jeanne will be holding horses for you in the woods."

"Where will they go from there?" André asked.

"A hunting lodge on my family's estate."

"But what will they do. Where will they go? They can't stay there forever," Jeanne asked.

"I don't really know." Jean said. "I imagine they will have to secretly sell most of their lands, inheritances, and any other possession of value. Their families will help. They will have to start a new life somewhere outside of France."

"*Mon Dieu*," André exclaimed, "Jean, with the French army fighting half of Europe outside of our borders and the French citizens in mob rule inside... where can they go?"

Jean thought a moment and said, "They might be able to go to England, but since we've been at war with them off and on for almost a hundred years, I doubt it would be very pleasant living conditions. They could take refuge there but they would be virtually ignored and shunned by everyone."

Jean thought for a second and then his eyebrows lifted,

"Maybe they could start a new life in Canada or Saint-Domingue, become plantation owners; anyway it is something they will have to work out later."

André thought about the options for a second and said, "Canada?" and shivered at the thought of living in that cold land. "No, not for me."

"You had better give it a second thought, André, in case this little trick of ours doesn't work and we have to make a quick exit. You had better turn some of your assets into francs in case you have to bribe yourself out of here and into another society," Jean said with all the sternness he could muster, trying to make sure André was thinking ahead.

The discussion of tomorrow's events and the working out of details went on well into the night before they went home.

Jean awoke early the next morning, after resting fitfully. The enormity of the day's events was gnawing at him and he wanted to get to the garrison so he could get the process started and, hopefully, settle his fears.

Jean usually walked to work because his house was only a few blocks from the garrison; but this morning he rode his horse in case he had to get some instructions to someone or somewhere quickly, or, God forbid, flee for his life.

Jean's horse turned the last corner and the massive military garrison came into view. As he approached it, he had that same feeling he always experienced upon seeing the garrison, the feeling of going into the mouth of the French military, where men waged battle and killed each other as a profession. He was always intimidated by the sternness of the grey stone walls, the shouting of orders, the sound of boots against the stone floors, and the general clatter of all the military paraphernalia. He usually hurried through it as fast as he could, so he could get to the familiarity of his hospital, but today he turned a different direction and headed for the military prison. He wanted to visit the prisoners as early as possible. That way he would draw much less attention to any of his actions by any latter arriving officers.

André was waiting for him and they walked toward the cell block. The guard was a little surprised at being visited by the inspecting doctor and the lieutenant of the execution squad so early in the morning.

"Open cell block four," Jean barked to the guard.

"Yes Sir," he said, fumbling for the keys.

The guard opened the massive wooden door and Dr. Formy-Duval, the inspecting doctor of condemned prisoners, walked in to examine the prisoners. He was supposed to write down their name and a general description of each condemned prisoner as well as any distinguishing marks for later body identification.

"Leave us," Jean instructed the guard. He did so and pulled the door behind him.

It took a moment for Jean's eyes to adjust to the dungeon's darkness punctuated by a single candle. As they adjusted, he saw Victor, Romain, and Jacques glumly looking at him from where they were sitting on some straw in the corner. In the other corner the fourth prisoner sat on the floor with his knees under his chin and his arms wrapped around his legs, rocking back and forth.

"So you have come to say goodbye to your old friends," Romain said.

Jean didn't say anything but walked over to where they were. They rose as he approached. Jean opened his arms and they all embraced.

41

Everyone started to talk at once, but Jean said, "Quiet, quiet, André and I don't have much time, so listen well. We have a plan worked out for your escape."

At this utterance there was much cheering and back slapping of Jean and André.

"You know a secret passage out of here, don't you Jean?" Jacques said with a wink.

"No, I don't," said Jean.

"You've bribed the guards?" said Victor.

"No!"

A concerned silence fell over the group and Romain said, "Well, what in God's name is going to happen?"

"Listen carefully; André has loaded the firing squads muskets with only gunpowder. When you have been marched out, blessed by the priest, and offered the blindfolds, which I want you to refuse, André will start the firing sequence." They all looked at André worriedly and then back to Jean. "I want you to put these blood bladders inside your shirt button nearest your heart. When the volley is fired, fall on the bladders so they will break open and stain your shirts. I will come up and check your pulse and pronounce you dead. André will be with me with his pistol. I may have him shoot one of you in the sleeve to make it look good. There *will* be a musket ball in his pistol. Now, his men will load you in a cart driven by Pierre, my brother, whom you all know. He will drive you into the country where Jeanne will have horses and further instructions for you."

They all thought about this for a minute and then Jacques, the mischievous one asked, "How come you don't want us to wear blindfolds?"

Jean rolled his eyes, "Because if a gun goes off accidentally, I don't want you all to fall down dead."

"Jean, isn't this a little dramatic? Isn't there another way?" asked Victor.

"I can't bribe the guards; there are too many Committee sympathizers among them, and believe me there is no secret passage out of here. Now, if you have any better ideas let me know and I will see if I can work them out in a couple of days," Jean said, becoming a little exasperated.

The three men looked at each other and finally nodded in agreement their acceptance of the plan, dramatic and dangerous as it was. They all took a deep breath and then the same thought struck all of them at once, the fourth prisoner.

All heads turned as one toward the fourth prisoner. The man had come out of his trance and it was evident that he had been listening to the escape plan.

"*Magnifique! Magnifique*, my friend!" said the man. "By this time tomorrow I might even be back in Paris with the polite society. By the way my name is Hippolyte Diderot of the Paris Diderots."

Jean felt a shudder go through his body. He knew of this Parisian family. They had been well-connected with the royal court and were well known for their brown nosing and being on constant look out to do the smallest of favors for the King. Even by the royal court standards they were looked upon as being silly and out of touch with reality.

Jean felt the only way to deal with Mr. Hippolyte Diderot was to be stern and he gathered up his toughest voice and said, "Let me assure you, Mr. Hippolyte Diderot, if you show up in Paris, you will be caught and guillotined and you will have signed a death warrant for all of us."

This hardly seemed to faze him. "Oh, not to worry," he said with an effeminate flip of his hand. "They won't catch me, I'm too smart for them."

This was too much for Victor, who stepped up and stood about six inches from Diderot's face. Jean thought Victor was going to choke him but Victor finally said, "If you are so smart, what are you doing here?"

"Oh, I'm here because you fellows were talking too loud at the tavern last night and they thought I was part of your group," Hippolyte said.

"Us? Too loud!" Victor sputtered.

Victor was so mad that he could barely talk. He reached for Hippolyte's throat but Romain put his hand on Victor's shoulder and stopped him.

Romain continued with what Victor wanted to say but could not get out, "It wasn't us shouting from table to table about the Committee's intelligence and calling them bitches. And then, for the love of God, you turn to our table and say, "Isn't that right fellows?" And then you turn to the rest of the tavern and introduce us as true defenders of the royal crown."

This retelling of the night's events was getting Victor, Romain, and Jacque's emotions too high. All three closed in to pound him.

Hippolyte knew when to give in so he threw up his hands and said, "All right, all right, maybe I was a little vocal."

"Damn right you were!" said Jacques.

Jean stepped in, and separated them, and said, "Let me explain this to you. You don't have much of a chance of being alive after ten o'clock this morning. If you don't take this seriously and cooperate, you will kill us all." Jean grabbed André's hand that held the pistol and pushed it right up Hippolyte's nose and said, "If I decide you can't handle it and you're going to get the rest of us killed, then I'll have André shoot you right now!"

Hippolyte seemed to have a revelation and quickly understood the seriousness of the situation and the men before him. He whimpered out, "Don't shoot; don't shoot me; I can do it."

"Good," said Jean.

Jean certainly hoped Hippolyte could, because if André had to shoot Hippolyte there was a good chance that Jean and André both would be pulled off the execution to go through an investigation and explain why they had to prematurely shoot a condemned prisoner and deprive the people of the pleasure of watching an execution of royalists.

They shoved Hippolyte back down on his straw bed and Jean went over the plan once again. He answered questions about the execution and the escape, as far as the escape was planned.

Jean and André left the prison wing and stepped out into the courtyard. They looked at each other with uncertainty and Jean said, "Stay with your men and try to keep them away from their muskets as long as possible." He took a deep breath. "See you at ten o'clock. God be with us."

André could only shake his head in agreement as he turned and they walked away from each other. "*Oui*", André said in a whisper. "He had better be, that's the only way it'll work."

A few minutes before ten o'clock Jean marched out to the parade ground with the commanding officer, his executive officer and a priest. Having a priest along could have been risky business in Paris, but a military garrison this far away would risk little, especially since the provinces were still deeply religious. The people expected to have the priest let the accused have one last chance to realize the error of their ways and die with the right ideals.

André had his men in two rows, flanking the prisoners, who were marching with their hands tied. He marched his men to the designated spot where there was a wooden wall behind them and a grassy spot to stand. André arranged the accused in a straight line and then had his men move to their firing positions about ten yards away.

Victor, Romain, and Jacques had the proper look of solemnity about them, but Hippolyte alternated between downright terror and smirky over-confidence.

The officer in charge stepped forward and read the charges. He was a young artillery officer recently transferred to the Paris-Le Harve area. His name was Captain Napoleon Bonaparte. "By order of the Citizen's Committee of LeHavre, responsible to the Grand Citizen's Committee in Paris, you have been ordered to be put to death by firing squad for your treasonous threats and expressions of loyalty to the former royal crown."

The crowd of civilians cheered at the statement. The man cheering and smiling the most was Claude Sartre, head of the local Citizen's Committee. Jean had disliked Claude almost from first glance. He was a weasel-looking man whose greatest thrill was watching people die, especially those he had helped condemn.

When the officer in charge returned to his place, the priest walked over to the condemned men and asked them for their confessions. Hippolyte confessed nothing and the priest blessed him. He then took one step to the right and said, "Victor, do you wish to confess?"

"Yes, Father, forgive all my sins of intention and those of omission I know not of," said Victor.

"My son, your sins are forgiven and you shall join Christ the son this day in heaven," the priest responded.

The priest took another step to the right and said, "Romain, do you wish to confess?"

"Yes, Father, forgive all my sins of intention and those of omission I know not of," said Romain.

"My son, your sins are forgiven and you shall join Christ the son this day in heaven," the priest said again.

He took a final step to the right and said, "Jacques, do you wish to confess?"

"Yes, Father," Jacques said solemnly. "If I fart too loudly when those muskets go off, please forgive me."

The priest was too stunned to say anything for a moment but regained his composure, smiled, and said, "Your sins are forgiven my son, and may your sense of humor serve you well in heaven with Christ."

The priest returned to his place in line and Captain Bonaparte looked toward André and said, "Lt. Dubois, carry out the execution."

André saluted the captain and turned to his squad and started the sequence. "Ready your arms." The soldiers put the muskets to their shoulders but did not sight. "Aim your musket." They sighted in their aim. André looked at his comrades' faces. They were standing there bravely but he could tell they were scared. One could never tell; maybe the soldiers checked their guns and reloaded them. André looked at Hippolyte and could see he was right before panicking. Hippolyte opened his mouth to say something, but André yelled, "Fire!" before Hippolyte could speak.

Victor, Romain, and Jacques all jerked backwards and twisted as they fell so they could break the blood bladder. Hippolyte was so shocked at the explosion of the volley that he fell to his knees and lingered there a long second before he fell over on his back.

André walked forward to the fallen and looked at them.

He looked toward Jean and motioned him over with his pistol. Now it was time for Jean to verify their death. He walked first to Hippolyte and knelt down. He put his hand over his heart and pushed to break the blood bladder. Hippolyte grunted. Jean whispered, "Shut up, you fool. Get ready to hear another gun shot." Jean stepped back and motioned to André to shoot Hippolyte. André stepped into position quickly and at the same time Jean stepped between André and the observing officers. André aimed the gun at Hippolyte's full sleeve and fired. Hippolyte jumped, but that only made it look like he took the impact of the bullet.

Jean leaned down again and whispered, "For God's sake, be still." He stood up and gave Hippolyte one last look. He almost smiled. Hippolyte was so stiff with terror he had lost control of his bladder and urinated. This helped with the illusion because most executed's muscles relax in death and released body wastes. After the excitement and drama of a second shot, Jean checked the other three, stood and faced the Captain in charge and said, "All dead, sir." The crowd cheered one last time. The Captain nodded and the officers and priest marched back to their quarters.

André motioned for Pierre to bring the cart over and told his men to load the bodies in the cart. Pierre had disguised himself well; he looked like any another country farmer with a horse and cart. The soldiers, anxious to get the task over with started tossing the bodies up in the wagon. Hippolyte's body was the last and when the two soldiers grasped him, one at his feet and one at his arms, one solder paused and looked at Jean, and said, "Doctor, this one is already stiff."

Jean thought quickly and said, "That's all right soldier, sometimes they stiffen their bodies at the moment of death and their muscles stay rigid for a few minutes."

They nodded their acceptance and tossed Hippolyte into the wagon as if he were a board.

Dr. Jean Formy-Duval signed the death certificates on the sideboard of the wagon.

André shouted to Pierre, "Move on, driver."

Pierre nodded and started the horse team and wagon and proceeded out the garrison gate. People ran along beside him looking at the executed officers in the wagon. After Pierre had gone a few blocks and most of the crowd had dispersed, he stopped and covered the men with a blanket.

Charles Patton

"Paris"

It took Pierre an hour to get into the countryside where he was to rendezvous with Jeanne. Once he covered up the bodies and left the city he did not have any more curious on-lookers. His passengers had been quiet throughout the journey with only an occasional grunt or a whispered question as to how much further. He had noticed they had pushed Hippolyte near the back of the wagon, away from the other three.

Pierre had made his last turn on the road which took him deep into the country and woods. It was an area near his family's isolated hunting lodge. The woods around it was filled with game and they would have no worries about food while they made further plans. Pierre could now see Jeanne up ahead with the horses.

"Whoa!" shouted Pierre to the horses. He gave Jeanne a mischievous smile and reached behind him and beat on the side of the wagon, jerked the blanket covering the men off and said, "Gentleman, be healed, arise and walk. This angel," pointing toward Jeanne, "has come to take possession of you." Pierre finished off with a big laugh at his joke.

The newly arisen sat up in the wagon looking disheveled and disorientated. Straw was all over their clothes and sticking out from their hair. They eased themselves out of the wagon and started working the kinks out of their stiff and sore bodies. Jeanne walked around with four horses and started hugging their necks with one arm while holding

50

the reins with the other. "Oh boys, I'm so glad everything worked and you are here safe." She turned to Pierre and asked, "Is Jean safe? Did they suspect anything?"

"No, it was as good as any play I ever saw. No one suspects a thing," Pierre said.

Jeanne smiled and turned to the men, "Jean wants you to use his family's hunting lodge for the next few days until you figure out where you will go. It's just over the hill and there are very few neighbors. I have stocked it well with provisions, but if you want to hunt for game you can. Be careful and stay deep in the woods."

Jacques was arching his back, trying to get the kinks out while listening to Jeanne. He straightened up, picked some straw out of his hair and said, "That's a good idea, madam, I think I'll stay here permanently and enjoy my resurrection here in Paradise Woods."

"No!" Jeanne said, "You must get out of the country. We cannot take any risks of any of you being recognized. Pierre is leaving immediately to contact your families and tell them of your situation. It has happened so fast that I don't think they know you were even arrested. They must arrange to get you money or jewels from the sale of your properties or your inheritance or something, but you must get out of the country and even then keep a low profile."

They were all nodding their reluctant agreement when Hippolyte spoke indignantly, "No, not me. I am leaving for Paris where my family will take care of me." Hippolyte reached for the reins of one of the horses when Romain grabbed his hand with one hand and grabbed his shirt by the other hand and lifted him up where only his toes were touching the ground.

"Listen, you little court flit, if you cause any one of us to get caught, the rest of us will hunt you down until we catch you. Do you understand me?" Hippolyte could only nod yes. "Do you believe me?" Romain shouted in his face.

"Yes, yes, I believe you," Hippolyte said almost crying.

Romain pulled Hippolyte close to his face where they were almost nose to nose and said, "You're not going anywhere until nightfall" and pushed him away and pointed a finger at him, "and you had better travel by night until you get to Paris."

This seemed to carry the point well and everyone mounted their horses and started for the hunting lodge. Jeanne walked over to the buckboard where Pierre was standing and said, "Jean was afraid this might happen. After you go to all the families and give them the news and instructions, he wants you to go to Paris and keep an eye on Hippolyte for a week or two. He wants to know that he's taking this seriously. Here's some money for expenses." She held out a bag full of coins to him.

Pierre shook his head no and said, "No, I don't need Jean's money. Tell him to spend it on my favorite sister-in-law and nephew. I have my own money that I'll spend in Paris."

Jeanne smiled and gave him a kiss on the cheek and thought to herself that Jean and Pierre were both good men. She imagined, had she not met Jean first, she could have easily fallen in love with Pierre. It had probably worked out for the best though. She didn't know if she could have put up with Pierre's roguish ways.

It took Pierre about a week to go to all the families and let them know what had happened and what must be done to help them. The families were distraught at first but relieved to know their sons were alive. They quietly started the process of raising money for their sons' escape and any new business venture they might endeavor.

After Pierre had visited the families, he returned to the Formy estate for his gentleman's clothes and a horse and carriage so he could follow in Hippolyte's circle without attracting undue attention. He also took an old hunting telescope so he could try to determine what was going on in the Diderot mansion.

After a week of travel he was on the street in front of the Diderot's home in Paris. He was trying to locate a rooming house nearby that would give him a view of the house and especially of the stable area so he could see anyone leaving or arriving. There was one boarding establishment three houses away, but it was on the wrong side of the house to see the stables. The view he needed was the one where a lady was sweeping her front porch. He tied his horse to the front gate and walked up to the lady on the porch.

Pierre took off his hat, bowed slightly, and said, "Pardon me mademoiselle, I'm looking for a comfortable room to stay in for a few weeks. The nature of my business leads me to this neighborhood, and I was wondering if you could recommend a nearby place to stay."

She stopped her work, took in what he had to say, thought for a moment, and cautiously said, "Madam Zola's boarding house is over there," pointing with her finger.

"Yes, I have already inspected her house, but I was looking for something a little less public."

The woman looked at him for a moment longer, as if she was doing a quick evaluation and said, "My mother occasionally rents a room in our house to acceptable gentlemen. If you like I will ask her if she will consider you. You understand, of course, she will be the one you have to persuade."

"Yes mademoiselle, I understand."

the back of the hand and said, "My pleasure, madam."

Charles Patton

"It is madam," she corrected, "My husband was killed last year in a military battle in Italy."

"Yes madam, I am very sorry about that."

"Wait here. I'll see if she will receive you."

Pierre turned and looked down the street and thought about the widow he had just been talking to. Wars and the present day executions puzzled and upset him. His brother had served as a surgeon in the French army in Italy and had only been posted back to France within the last year. He wondered if Jean had performed surgery on her husband. He could picture his brother, trying his best under battlefield conditions to save him, but in vain.

The door opened and the woman motioned Pierre to come in, "Please, come in. My mother is in the parlor and would like to meet you. My name is Colette. Please, may I have your name so I may introduce you to my mother?"

"Pardon me, Madam Colette. My name is Pierre Formy." he said with a slight bow and walked through the door all at the same time.

When Pierre entered the parlor he could tell this had been an elegant house at one time but was now suffering from neglect, not physical neglect but financial neglect. The place was clean and all was in order, but he could see areas where furniture had once been and was now gone, possibly sold. Pierre could already perceive what was happening with a father dead and a husband killed.

"Mother, this is the gentleman that is interested in renting the upstairs room for a few weeks. His name is Pierre Formy," she said pausing, giving Pierre a chance to bow toward her, "and this is my mother, Madam Balzac."

Pierre took Madam Balzac's outstretched hand and performed the customary bow combined with kissing the back of the hand and said, "My pleasure, madam."

Madam Balzac looked over Pierre a moment and then spoke, "My daughter says we should rent you the room upstairs. You look like a fine man with a gentlemanly manner, so I will leave that decision and any financial matters to my daughter who will show you the room and the house." She struggled out of the chair with the help of her cane and started walking out of the room when she stopped, turned, and said, "She rules the house now." With a chuckle she said, while walking away, "and if she takes a liking to you I'm sure she can be most entertaining."

"Mother!"

Pierre looked down at his feet, trying not to laugh and also trying not to further embarrass Colette by looking at her face for the moment.

"Please, Monsieur Formy follow me and I will show you the room." Colette said, her voice still full of emotion. "I swear, old people and children don't care what they say."

Perfect, thought Pierre as he looked out the window of the room Colette was showing him. It had an excellent view of the side entrance and stable where all the people coming to the Diderot house had to enter.

"This room will do fine. What is the cost?" Pierre asked.

"Ten francs a week and if you will help buy some food you may eat with us."

"If I pay you twenty francs a week will that suffice for room and board?"

"Oh, sir, that is more than generous!" She had wanted to decline such a generous offer and settle on fifteen instead, but they needed the money and if he had it to spare she would take it.

"Fine, I'll put my horse and carriage at the stable down the street and bring my clothes back and unpack." He was glad to close the deal with such a perfect viewpoint and with so lovely a host.

The evening had gone well and he had a pleasant meal with the two ladies and their servant who was maid, housekeeper, and cook all in one. Times were hard in Paris and their maid took care of the two ladies, and the house for the privilege of living and eating there, and maybe only a pittance of a wage. They had inquired into the nature of his business and he had made up some story about checking out possible investments for his employer. The business was taverns and night entertainment which might mean he would be gone until late at night. He wanted to give himself as much latitude as possible with his hosts so they didn't become suspicious.

He was presently using the telescope, looking into the windows of the Diderot house trying to spot Hippolyte or wait until he visited, possibly in disguise. He would have to be alert.

He stayed up until two o'clock in the morning and saw nothing, except one time when he thought he saw Hippolyte go by one of the windows, but he couldn't be sure. The lighting was poor and the image was fleeting, but still he had that same walk and the way he carried himself was familiar.

Pierre kept a watchful eye over the Diderot mansion for the next few days and it did not take long before he started seeing Hippolyte. He could tell Hippolyte was getting restless in the house. The first full day Pierre had watched the house Hippolyte had come outside in the back yard, in full view of all neighboring houses, and had walked around for a good half hour. The second day he had gone for a walk in the neighborhood in disguise. Pierre had followed

Centaur of the Savannahs

at a discreet distance and nothing of any importance had happened, but Pierre could tell Hippolyte was not only getting braver but more careless. Today he had gone for a walk and had eaten a discrete lunch with some friends. Pierre had taken a table nearby where he could hear parts of the conversation, and he was sure they were planning a night out.

Pierre, anticipating the night to come, had gotten his carriage and horse and hitched it outside the Balzac house. After the evening meal he had positioned himself in the parlor where he could see the Diderot house and talked to Madam Balzac and Colette. Pierre enjoyed the conversation so much that nine o'clock came before he realized it. He quickly broke off the conversation, which both surprised and upset Colette, and went up to his room. He felt like he would have noticed if anyone had come to the Diderot house, but he was enjoying himself too much and had to get into a position to concentrate on his target. He felt it would not be long before Hippolyte's friends would come for him if they were going to come at all.

At nine-thirty, two men in a large carriage pulled up to the Diderot house and Hippolyte climbed in. He was in disguise but Pierre could easily pick him up now, whatever the disguise.

Pierre quickly rushed downstairs, out the door and into his carriage so he would not lose them. As he was leaving, he caught a glimpse of Colette watching him with a quizzical look on her face.

A little after ten o'clock they arrived at a tavern known for their risqué shows and questionable clientele. He gave them a few minutes to get inside and settled before he entered.

The tavern was all his mother had ever told him to stay away from. Half-naked women were on the stage, men

57

drooled in their ale, and people of the same sex snuggled against each other.

He positioned himself at a point on the bar where he could be inconspicuous yet keep an eye on Hippolyte and his friends. The evening went by with Hippolyte and his friends having a big party with much laughter and almost no attempt at keeping a low profile. Pierre watched the rest of the crowd to see if anyone was paying any particular attention to Hippolyte's group.

After a while his attention focused on another table with three men. Two of them were completely engrossed in the show and the girls on the stage. One of them only spent part of his time looking at the girls on stage. The rest of the time his attention was on Hippolyte's table. There was something vaguely familiar about this person but Pierre could not quite put his finger on it.

Pierre was trying to assess the situation when one of the bar girls came up and leaned on his back and rested her chin on his shoulder and said, "You look like you could use some company."

Pierre could smell the perfume before she spoke. He half turned and when he did, her chin left a patch of makeup on his jacket shoulder. "Uh, no, mademoiselle, I'm afraid I cannot tonight."

She did not let the refusal stop her and made an attempt to brush the makeup off his shoulder. "What's the matter? Don't you like me?" she said, with a dimpled smile.

Pierre was tempted. This was a good-looking girl, better than anything he had ever seen back in the provinces, but if he accepted her invitation, he would have to leave the tavern and as brazen as Hippolyte was getting, there was no telling what could happen. He took a deep breath. "I'm sorry, as much as I would like to and as pretty as you are, I can't tonight; maybe next time."

She turned to walk away but paused long enough to say, "You might not get a next time."

He raised a glass as a salute to her. "My loss."

Pierre turned his attention back to Hippolyte and his friends and saw that they were leaving. He looked away so Hippolyte would not see him staring at him. His gaze fell on the man who had also been looking at Hippolyte. The man's eyes followed Hippolyte out the door and then a look of recognition came over the man and he clasped his hands in front of his chest, smiled, and said something as if in amazement. Pierre knew Hippolyte had been recognized, but who was this man. The man looked familiar but he couldn't place him. He waited about five minutes, left the tavern, and went back to the Balzac's house.

As Pierre was walking to the door at the boarding house, he could not help but think that something was about to happen with Hippolyte. A man had recognized him and for some reason was amazed. He was in such deep thought when he came through the door, he did not see Colette waiting for him and he almost bumped into her.

"My, isn't our mind occupied?" she said with a touch of sarcasm. She took a step closer to him and sniffed the perfume which had lingered on his clothes. Her gaze went to his shoulder were the makeup was still there and started brushing it away with her fingers. "Did we have fun?"

He knew exactly what she was thinking and suddenly it was important for him to convince her that he had done nothing wrong. "Colette, this is my job to check out night spots and taverns for my employer." He paused for a second to get a reading on her face and decided to see if he could get her to laugh. "Besides I assure you that my celibacy is intact."

Colette stared at him for another few seconds without changing expressions, just long enough to let him struggle without the knowledge of being believed or not. She finally decided he was probably telling the truth and said, "I doubt that, Monsieur Formy." She turned and walked up the stairs with as much movement as she could manage in her derriere without looking ridiculous.

Pierre took a deep breath, leaned against the wall, and watched her as she ascended the stairs. He thought, *You're torturing me.* He waited a moment until Colette disappeared, pushed off the wall, and started up the stairs.

Pierre sat in the chair by the window overlooking the Diderot mansion. He was undressing and was down to his underwear when he picked up his telescope and sat down in his chair to look at some activity in Hippolyte's window. The telescope was a well-used hunting scope and had long ago lost its tightness between telescoping sections when fully extended. He could open and close it with one hand by either tilting it up or down. He must have sat there a half an hour, thinking about the situation at the tavern tonight and looking through the telescope. The man who recognized Hippolyte bothered Pierre. He knew the face was familiar but who was it? He tried to concentrate on the problem, but Colette's mesmerizing stair climbing act kept interrupting his concentration.

Pierre had just closed the scope by collapsing it and leaned back in his chair when he noticed light shoot under his door from the hall lantern. The light was soft and fanned out under the door. In a few seconds his door latch turned and the door opened slowly. Colette stood in the doorway. Pierre was captivated by the effect. The soft back light of the hall lantern showed Colette in silhouette through her thin gown. Her breasts were particularly full and the back lighting effect showed them off with great effect. Their eyes locked and Pierre leaned forward. When he leaned forward, the telescope he was holding in his lap tilted down and extended to its fullest extent. Pierre was embarrassed by this apparent phallic gesture, but when Colette smiled with amusement, he recovered and said, "Madam, you do have an amazing effect on both man and machine."

Pierre stood up from the chair and they walked into each other's arms and started kissing passionately. Pierre laid her down on the bed and broke from the passionate kisses long enough to say, "I hoped you would come, I..."

Colette put her fingers to his lips to hush him and said, "Shhh, don't say anything." She paused and as she started to resume the embrace she said, "I just hope you work as well as your telescope."

After Pierre and Colette made love, they talked long into the night about themselves and Pierre disclosed his true mission in Paris. Colette stayed with him until about four o'clock in the morning. Pierre was exhausted and slept until about eight-thirty and was awakened by a clatter outside his window. He stumbled to the window and could see several policemen rushing into the Diderot's house. There were two men in civilian dress who appeared to be high officials. One of them looked like he might be the same person Pierre saw at the nightclub.

Colette came rushing into his room to tell him about the scene next door, but when she saw that Pierre was already observing it, she joined him at the window.

In a few minutes two policemen came out holding on to Hippolyte. He was dressed only in his nightgown and robe. They unceremoniously dumped him into a carriage and left with him. The two supervisors turned to congratulate each other. They shook hands and continued talking for a bit. The man Pierre was eyeing through his telescope took off his hat, and looked up at the sky, giving Pierre a full face view of him. Then it struck him.

"It's Claude Sartre, head of the Citizen's Committee in LeHavre. I should have known. What's he doing in Paris?" he said in amazement.

"Well, whatever he's doing here, you had better beat him back to LeHavre," Colette said.

The two men finished talking and took the reins of their horses from the house servant and rode off in the same direction of the carriage carrying Hippolyte.

"I'm going to see what I can find out," Colette said and ran out of the room.

Pierre started getting dressed and was putting on his shoes when he saw Colette walk to the servant who had held the men's reins. He and Colette must have known each other because he welcomed her warmly and they talked for several minutes.

Pierre was packing his bags when Colette came in the door and said, "I was just talking to Alex, their servant, and he said Hippolyte was spotted at a tavern last night and one of those two men recognized him. He also said the two men had many questions. Like, how could he not die at the firing squad, are the other three alive also, and most important, why had the doctor signed the death certificates?" Colette paused to get her breath and then continued, "He said they were going to the authorities and immediately dispatch some soldiers to LeHavre and arrest everyone involved with the execution."

Pierre tightened the cinch on his bag and stood up straight, looked at Colette and said, "Colette, you know I have to leave immediately to warn my brother and his friends."

"Yes, yes, I know. You must go immediately."

"As soon as this is settled, you know I will return for you."

Colette had heard such promises before. Finally, she said, "I pray you do."

Pierre grabbed her with his free arm, pulled her to him, and kissed her. "I mean it." He released her and hurried out of the house to hitch up his horse and carriage. Colette followed him to the stable and watched as he hitched the horse. He jumped in the carriage and looked at Colette, "I'll write," was all he could get out. Colette could only nod and wave as he rode away.

Claude Sartre was having a good morning and was feeling especially good about himself. He had been called to Paris by the famous Robespierre to be given acclaim and recognition for his good works in LeHavre. He was to be taken around Paris and introduced to all the right people as being the type of man who best personified France's democratic principles and as a person who was virtuous in executing France's decadent society. This was all done as a reward for his latest accomplishments in helping clean out France's military of royalist sympathizers.

Now he had added to his stature by uncovering a plot where people had obviously tricked the government and escaped execution. He wondered if he would be blamed for this person's escape, but he dismissed the thought. Surely the military would get the blame.

He was now waiting in an outer office of the famous Robespierre and would soon be called in to have his moment of glory for all his accomplishments.

The inner door opened. Robespierre walked out, greeted Claude warmly, and said, "Monsieur Sartre, at last we meet, I have heard so many good things about you and your work in LeHavre."

"Thank you, thank you, I'm very happy to serve France in such a manner," Claude said.

"Please come into my office and we'll discuss these new circumstances," Robespierre said.

Claude followed Robespierre into his office and sat down in a chair across from his desk. The office was sparsely furnished and did not give off any royalist airs. This pleased Claude.

Robespierre watched Claude as he looked around his office. He needed people like Claude Sartre. Someone who could act as a personal spy in the provinces of France and develop spheres of influence and let him know what was going on in the cities outside of Paris. He needed to flatter Sartre, to ensure his loyalty, not to France, but to him, Robespierre.

"Claude, tell me, how did you manage to find and catch this person who escaped his own execution?" Robespierre asked.

"Well, Monsieur, no one suspected a thing. It was cleverly done. I was in the tavern last night and recognized Monsieur Diderot despite his disguise. This morning I told my story to the authorities and they took me to his house, for identification purposes, and arrested him. It was all very simple, sir," Claude said with false modesty.

"But how did they manage to fake the execution?" asked Robespierre.

"The military might be involved, maybe even the Captain in charge of the firing squad." said Claude.

"Yes, maybe, although I doubt it. The doctor who signed

the death certificates, what about him?" asked Robespierre.

"Yes, he must be in on it, since he signed the death certificates," said Claude.

Robespierre leaned forward and said, "Monsieur Sartre, I feel I must entrust this investigation to you, and that you can find out every last detail and see that justice is carried out."

Claude swelled with pride and importance and said, "Nothing will stop me. I will go to any length to find out the truth and carry out justice. Whatever it takes or wherever I have to go. I will be your servant of justice."

Robespierre knew this was going to work out well. This was a good story, one where the hated royalist seemed to have escaped justice, only to be brought back by fate and dogged determination by one of his committee members.

"Monsieur Sartre, I hereby give you the authority to investigate this matter and carry out any execution necessary. Do not fail me," Robespierre said. "Great things await you."

They both rose and shook hands. Claude said, "I will not fail. I will pursue until death."

Claude left the office with a feeling of direction and importance that he had never felt before in his life. He had a mission to fulfill and nothing would stop him.

Charles Patton

"Pursuit"

Jean was resting in a chair in front of the fireplace at his home in LeHavre. It had been a hard month emotionally since the execution and two weeks since Pierre had left. The flames of the fireplace danced for him and he couldn't take his eyes off them. He could feel his mind slowing down and his muscles relaxing in the fire's warmth. He felt like he had been riding a wild horse for over a month now and the horse was only now coming under control and beginning a gentle walk. It had been such a gamble with all their lives, then the exhilaration and excitement at their success, and then back to constant worry about whether their feat would remain undetected or not.

Jean had made a few late afternoon and evening trips to the lodge where his friends were hiding to check on their progress. The families were providing financial help for their future endeavors, but Jean found that he constantly had to guide their thinking about their future destination. The main destination topics were Canada and Saint-Domingue (Haiti), but they would often go off on a tangent about Morocco, Ghana, the South Pacific and even America.

Jean exclaimed to them, "Men, think about this. This is not some wild adventure. Your wives and children will be joining you soon. What kind of education will they get on some South Sea island?"

"I can't think of any place but France for an education for our children," said Romain.

"Look, Canada has 200,000 Frenchmen and Saint-Domingue has 30,000 Frenchmen. At least there your children will know about French culture and language, and by the time they're ready for higher education you can send them back to France," said Jean.

The idea that this was a temporary thing and they might return to France at a later date always seemed to bring them to their senses. Just stay in a French culture for a few years and then return.

Jean doubted this would ever happen. Once established in a new country they would probably establish a business venture that would be more successful than anything they could do here. In France they would either stay in the military or live off their family's wealth.

Jeanne brought him out of his trance by bringing him some hot spiced tea. "Here, *cheri*, have some tea," she said. She snuggled down in his lap and asked, "How were the boys doing at the hunting lodge today?"

"Oh, they're fine. I think they have sorted out their situation and are making choices where to go. Their families have all managed to get them money and jewels," he said.

"What about their wives and children? Have they seen them?" she asked.

"No, that's too risky right now. They'll join them after they get settled in their new countries. Wherever that's going to be," he said.

"Haven't they decided yet?" she asked.

"No, but they have narrowed down to Canada or Saint-Domingue," he said.

The conversation paused for a moment while they gazed into the fire and then Jean asked, "How's your little project coming along?"

Charles Patton

"You mean my little sewing project? Well, it's nearly finished. I have sewn all the jewels into the lining of my dresses and certain undergarments", she said raising one eyebrow mischievously, "and I have taken a large sock and tied strings around the top and bottom so I can fasten the strings around my neck and the bottom strings around my waist".

"Good, it will be a good place to put the gold coins. I have converted most of our property into gold so they should be good anywhere we might be forced to go."

"Do you really think they will find us out? It's been over two weeks now," she asked.

"I don't know. It depends on that idiot Hippolyte," Jean said with his anger rising. He paused a moment and let his emotions subside and continued, "If the worst happens, then we will have to move quickly and it's better to be ready and have everything planned."

"Would we still go to Saint-Domingue?"

"If we manage to escape, yes, that's where the family plantation is located. My father started the plantation several years ago and has an overseer running it. He has kept it a secret though. He didn't want anyone in the royal court to know that our wealth is from a sugar plantation and not old money." Changing moods he said, "We would be sugar plantation royalty, living in the sunny Caribbean with all the servants you would ever need," Jean said in jest.

Jeanne smiled and said, "Sounds nice, although I'm not too much on house servants being constantly under foot. Just a little help is all I'll need."

"Whatever you want, Princess, whatever you want," Jean said.

Jeanne was scoffing at Jean's humor when she was startled by someone pounding on the door. They looked toward the door as it flew open and Pierre stood there. He looked exhausted.

He leaned on the door frame and said, "Hippolyte was arrested yesterday in Paris. I drove the horse and carriage as hard as I could. I've killed one horse and I don't know if the one I've have now is going to make it or not. Anyway, I think it will be tomorrow afternoon before soldiers get here to arrest you and the others. You have to go, now!"

Jean jumped up to steady Pierre and help him to a seat. Jeanne gave him something to drink and Pierre filled them in on the details as he rested in the chair. Pierre told them all that had happened in Paris.

Jean asked, "Pierre do you think you can help Jeanne load a few trunks on the carriage and take her to the lodge?"

"Sure but where are you going?" Pierre asked.

"Down to the docks, to find a couple of sea captain friends of mine. I have to make some arrangements," said Jean.

"When will you join me at the lodge?" Jeanne asked.

"Tomorrow, about noon. I have to make some purchases first thing tomorrow morning."

"Don't we have everything we need? You don't need to be out in public anymore."

"Yes, I know, but I need to throw a red herring on our trail to mislead anyone who might search for us," explained Jean.

"How are you going to do that?"

"I'm going to buy some clothes and equipment for cold weather, to make people think we're going to Canada," said Jean. "I'll buy them first thing in the morning and then come on out to the lodge."

"You're cutting it awfully close, my brother. The

soldiers could be here by noon tomorrow," Pierre said.

"I know, but it needs to be done," Jean answered.

The Captain's Table was a tavern patronized by ship owners and sea captains alike. It was a tavern where the common sailor did not go because it was not conducive to a good time with all the management around. Here owners of ships found captains and captains found ships to command. This was also the place to find cargo for one's ship or vice-versa.

On the way to the tavern Jean saw André and briefed him on the bad news. They walked through the door with their hats pulled down almost over their eyes and their collars up on their coats. Although they were not in disguise, they weren't in military uniform either. They were trying to blend in with the patronage. Jean was looking for two men who were sea captains whom he had heard were in town. He had known these men for years and knew he could trust them. He knew they had the same sentiments about the present government that he had.

He looked around the room and let his eyes adjust to the dim light. Finally he saw them, Captain Racine and Captain Chenier, at a booth on the far side of the room. He walked over to join them. When he stopped at their table they looked up and recognized Jean. They started to stand and make a big fuss over him, but Jean hushed them down with his hands, introduced André, and sat down with them.

"Jean, you ole sea dog, how are you doing?" Captain Racine asked, "We were talking about you earlier, with you living here in the harbor town of LeHavre."

"Quietly, quietly, gentlemen", Jean said getting them to lower their voices.

"Captain Racine, Captain Chenier, I'm in trouble and I

need your help," Jean said.

"What's the matter Jean? You know we'll help," said Captain Racine.

"I'm counting on it. Captain Racine, I understand that your ship the *L'Emmanuel* is going to Saint-Domingue via the Canary Islands in two days, and Captain Cheneir I believe yours is going to Canada later the same day," said Jean.

"That's true, Jean, it's like a regular family reunion. We haven't seen each other in two years and now we're running almost side by side for two ports running," said Captain Chenier.

"Good," said Jean, "that's what I thought. Now here's what's happening."

Jean related the whole story over the next hour while they had dinner. It was as if he was telling them the story of a dramatic play and their expressions showed it. When he had finished, Captain Racine asked, "What can we do?"

Jean took a deep breath and started, "This is the way I want to do it. Captain Chenier, we want to leave on your ship for Canada and then secretly switch ships in the Canary Islands and head on out for Saint-Domingue. We will place luggage on both ships. After the *Le Bordeaux* departs for Canada, divide the clothes and equipment among the sailors to buy their silence. We will board your ship tomorrow just before it leaves. If we are not there, leave without us and pick us up twenty-five miles down the coast off Cape d'Antifer. You'll have to get us in row boats."

Jean paused and looked at the two men. They were captivated and amazed.

Chenier finally spoke with a little uncertainty in his voice, "This is amazing. You certainly live a dramatic life."

"Don't worry Jean. We'll help you." said Captain Racine.

"Thank you, gentleman. Yes, it's more dramatic than I care for, but it is something neither my family nor myself can maintain for long. It's like burning a candle at both ends."

"Jean, when you send your luggage to my ship, send it all to my ship, *Le Bordeaux*. I'll have some of my men secretly take the luggage for Saint-Domingue the *L'Emanuel* a few hours later, in case someone is watching, or is questioned later." said Captain Chenier.

"Thanks Captains," Jean said shaking their hands. "I'll see you soon."

When they walked outside, Jean said, "André, go pack your things and come spend the night with me. We need to get an early start tomorrow on our purchases and then go to the lodge. You need to send a message to the garrison that you are ill and will not be there tomorrow. I have already done so earlier this evening."

"Yes, Jean", said André. He could hardly say anything else. He felt like he was in a dream and maybe this was not really happening to him. "I'll be at your house in a couple of hours."

Jean and André awoke early the next morning, but they did not hurry out to the market place because the shops they wanted to visit would not be open until about mid-morning. Instead they spent a couple of hours discussing the escape plans over an extended breakfast. Jean used this time to talk to André about what they were about to embark on, in hopes of enhancing André's confidence level and try to get his outlook changed from fright and pessimism to anticipation and adventure.

As they rode their horses to market, Jean could see André was in better spirits and maybe his little talk had helped.

"Here is Dumont's outfitters store. Shall we purchase supplies here?" asked André.

"Yes, this is a good store to buy from."

Yes, Jean thought to himself, *This is where I'm going to throw down my red herring. It should create confusion when they start asking questions about us.*

He would buy the store owner's silence with a small tip. He knew about this particular man and was sure that he would easily sell them out or cave in under only a slight amount of pressure.

"Gentlemen," shouted the merchant. "What can I help you with today?"

"Sir, we are going on an expedition to find our fortune in some far overseas land. We will need supplies to keep us alive in the coldest of temperatures and the most difficult of places," Jean said.

"Ah, Canada, huh," the old merchant said.

Jean smiled and held up his hands to quiet him down and show that he wanted to keep it all under wraps.

"How many people?" the store owner asked.

"About a dozen," Jean replied.

The store owner's eyebrows arched slightly. *This could be a tidy little sale*, he thought.

They spent about forty-five minutes collecting items for cold weather and trapping. Jean paid the owner and gave him a small amount extra "You never saw us." Jean said, as he laid the extra francs in the merchant's hand and started walking out the door.

"*Oui, monsieur*, I don't even know what day it is today." The merchant said as he turned back to put the money in his cash drawer, all the time thinking that for such a small silence bribe he might be able to sell the information in the future.

Jean and André hired a wagon on the street and instructed the driver to take the merchandise to the ship *Le Bordeaux.*

As the wagon left, André asked, "Jean, shouldn't I go with him? He could sell all our supplies before he reaches the docks."

"Don't worry about it André. If he delivers it, fine. If he doesn't, then no loss. We will never use it. It's all a diversionary tactic," Jean said, patting André on the shoulder.

They made a few other stops to buy small items plus a stop at a medicine shop. They bought supplies that they would really need but threw in a few extra purchases of special and exotic medicines for pneumonia.

They mounted their horses and Jean said, "Let's head for the lodge. Sartre and his men will be here soon."

As they rode to the outskirts of town, André was laughing at how Sartre would be fooled by their tricks. As they joked about it, a dozen or so riders, mostly military, came around a curve. They were tired and dusty and looked like they had ridden hard. There was one civilian in particular who looked like he didn't care how far he had to go. He was going to get there.

Jean and André looked at each other with knowing recognition of Sartre and his militia. They held their head down, trying to cover their face with their hats, and at the same time try to look as casual and inconspicuous as possible when they passed. They tried not to lock eyes with anyone, especially Sartre, but it was hard not to look at the face of the man who wanted you dead.

When the militia was out of sight, they spurred their horses and pushed hard for the lodge.

Jeanne was sitting on the front porch steps watching Louis play in the yard when she heard horses approaching. She gathered Louis in her arms and stood watching until she recognized Jean and André.

She turned her head toward the lodge and shouted, "Jean and André are coming!"

Victor, Romaine, and Jacques came running out.

Jean reined to a stop, jumped off, and gave Jeanne and Louis a kiss and took him from her arms. Louis responded with a laugh.

Romaine, Victor, and Jacques surged forward and Victor asked, "What's the situation, Jean? When do we leave?"

Jean handed Louis back to his mother and said, "The situation is worsening. Sartre and the militia are already in town. In fact I think we passed them on the road." Everyone gasped at the revelation. "Don't worry, they didn't realize who we were, obviously."

"Is passage arranged?" asked Jacques.

"Yes, it is," answered Jean, "We'll try to sneak into the docks tomorrow morning. We are to leave on the *Le Bordeaux*, tomorrow, on the afternoon tide. The *Le Bordeaux* is headed for the Canarys and then on to Canada. We'll swap ships at Los Palmayes in the Canary Islands. From there we'll take the *L'Emanuel* to Saint-Domingue."

"Let's go inside and I'll fill you in on all the details," Jean said. For the next two hours Jean explained and laid out the plan for their escape, which included all the diversionary tactics they had taken to make Sartre think they were going to Canada.

Pierre was riding hard for the lodge. He had left LeHavre only an hour before and was coming up the road to the lodge. All afternoon he had been watching the docks where the *L'Emanuel* and *Le Bordeaux* were docked. Sartre and his men were on the docks by early afternoon asking questions about Jean and André. They were also interested in all ships and their destinations.

Pierre followed Sartre as close as he could without becoming obvious. He could not get close enough to hear but he could tell by the animated gestures of the participants if they were having any success or not. Some people seemed to indicate that they had seen Jean and André on the docks. This wasn't true of course, but it made Sartre suspicious enough to post several guards on the docks, especially at the location of the *L'Emanuel* and *Le Bordeaux* which were docked in the same section of the harbor. These ships were prime suspects because they were leaving soon and were going to Saint-Domingue and Canada, two prime locations for escaping Frenchmen.

Pierre knew his brother and friends were planning to come to the docks tomorrow morning and he had to warn them. He rode hard for the lodge. When he arrived he dismounted, almost on the run, and ran into the lodge.

Jean looked up from the table. "Pierre, what is it?"

"Sartre has posted guards at the docks. You can't go into LeHavre tomorrow."

Everyone let out a groan and looked at Jean.

Jean waited for a moment and said, "We'll use our alternate plan, as discussed, with the Captain Racine. If we don't show up, they will pick us up off Cape d'Antifer."

"That's twenty-five miles down the coast," said Romaine. We will have to get everyone in the wagons and reach Cape d'Antifer by mid-afternoon to make the tide.

That's about three miles an hour if we leave early tomorrow morning."

"Sounds about right," said Jean. "Our luggage is already aboard and our wagons will not be slowed by excess baggage, but we will have to get up at four o'clock tomorrow morning and be on the road by first light. It will take us until early afternoon to reach Cape d'Antifer and we dare not be late. High tide is at four o'clock. Everyone pack now and be ready to load before daybreak."

Jeanne was choking on the dust from the road as they traveled. She put a thin layer of gauze over Louis's face as he slept to keep the dust from bothering him. Jean, who hardly slept during the night, had awakened everyone a little before first light. The wagon she rode on bounced her and Louis but it seemed to act as a rocking motion to little Louis. Jean was riding the horse he had owned for years. He could have sold him many times but the horse was more than a piece of property to him, he was a friend and until now he was not for sale.

Jeanne watched her husband on his horse and then noticed his face. He was tired. They had been up several hours but he looked exhausted. They were all tired from this ordeal but Jean, as always, carried the responsibility on his shoulders and everyone looked to him for the final decision. She hoped they would be on the ship by nightfall and maybe then he would allow himself to rest.

"Jean," she called to him. He slowly turned his head toward her and she smiled at him and formed a kiss on her lips. He smiled, winked, and seemed to gain strength as he straightened in the saddle.

I have to get them on the ship no matter what happens to me, he thought. The morning had been without incident but every minute seemed to go by in slow motion. They were being dragged down by alternating fears of not reaching the ship and fear of what their lives might be like in a primitive and foreign land.

"Are we making good time?" Jeanne asked him.

"Yes," he said. "Things have gone almost too well; let's hope our luck holds. We should reach Cape d' Antifer by mid-afternoon if we keep up this pace." But Jean was still worried. If Sartre were to somehow get on their trail they could be easily tracked. They were not an unusual sight, a caravan of two wagons filled with baggage, and six men on horseback. They would not have been a sight where farmers would have dropped their hoes and stared, but it was unusual enough to take note of and would be easily remembered if someone asked about them.

Sartre surveyed the shops and markets as he gazed down the main street leading to the docks. He spent most of the morning asking various outfitters and shop owners if they had seen anyone fitting Jean and André's description, but no luck. Yesterday had been more productive. Several people they questioned seemed to think they had seen Dr. Formy-Duval on the docks. If true, then it confirmed Sartre's suspicion that Dr. Formy-Duval was trying to escape on one of the ships in the harbor. Most likely the *Le Bordeaux*, since it was headed to Canada. But, the people he questioned might be telling him what they thought he wanted to hear. Some people were too eager to please members of The Committee.

"Now there's a likely shop." Sartre said, pointing out a store to the two soldiers with him. It was a trader's shop which specialized in equipment and hardware needed in foreign lands.

Sartre walked into the store followed by two soldiers which attracted the store owner's attention.

"Gentlemen, can I help you?" the owner asked.

"Yes, we are searching for two dangerous traitors who may be trying to flee France. One is a tall, distinguished man, dark hair and eyes, about twenty-five to thirty years old. The other man is younger, medium height, with sandy blond hair."

The old store owner's eyes immediately lit up. These were the two gentlemen about whom he recently had suspicions. He had been right. There might be a further profit in this after all.

"Would there be a reward for the information about these two gentlemen?" he asked.

Sartre could tell by the way the man's eyes lit up that he knew something.

"The only reward you'll get is the cutting edge of the guillotine if you hide information from a member of The Committee," Sartre said.

At the mention of The Committee the old man froze in terror and then started blurting out all he knew. "Yes, yes, those two men came in yesterday and bought a great deal of equipment. They were going to Canada. All the gear was for cold weather."

"Did they take the merchandise with them or did they have you deliver it somewhere?" Sartre asked.

"Um..., I believe they hired a wagon and took off with it."

"What kind of horses did they have?"

"I don't know, I didn't see where they went after we loaded the supplies."

"Anything else we should know?" asked Sartre.

"No, no, that's all I know."

Sartre and the two soldiers walked out the door and as they walked away he stopped and pointed at one of the soldiers. "Check all the wagons from here to the docks and see if you can find the wagon he hired and where he delivered the goods". He turned to the other soldier, "Check all the medicine shops between here and the docks. If I were going on a long trip, I know I would buy medicines. Both of you, meet me at the garrison at noon with your results."

It was almost noon and Sartre stood on the street across from the docks where *Le Bordeaux* was anchored. He was waiting for his men to arrive when the port master approached him. The port master was a jolly but sly old sailor who had done well by knowing which political end was up.

"Good day, Monsieur Sartre," the port master said, tipping his hat. "I am the harbor port master and I have heard of your situation and I would like to offer my assistance."

Sartre wasn't really in a mood for conversation. He wanted to talk to his men as soon as they arrived and find out if they had made any new discoveries. He would have brushed off anyone else but the word, "port master" made him realize that it might be to his advantage to talk to this man. He actually might be of assistance.

"Good day, port master, thank you for your concern," Sartre said. "The best assistance you can give me is by telling me where Dr. Formy-Duval and his friends are."

"Ha!" the port master laughed. "If I knew that I would have already told you. I do not keep secrets from The Committee, besides the whole city is talking about you and Dr. Formy-Duval. Well, don't worry sir; he can't stay hidden for long in this city."

"Well, he seems to have disappeared. He's either already left by ship or is not in LeHavre," Sartre said.

"Sir," the port master injected. "Have you considered that the Doctor and his friends might be at their family's hunting lodge a few miles north of town?"

"No, I haven't been told about it," Sartre said. "Do you know where the lodge is?"

"No, I don't, but anyone living northeast of town should know the location. They are a prominent family and have large land holdings," answered the port master.

"Thank you, thank you very much." Sartre said as he saw his two soldiers coming toward him. He knew he had to take quick action to cut the doctor's escape plan off.

Sartre had a quick conference with his men and found out that although they could not find the wagon which took the supplies, one soldier did find an apothecary shop owner who remembered the doctor and reported that he bought medicines for cold weather conditions, pneumonia in particular.

"Let's go to the garrison and get the rest of the detail and take the road heading northeast out of town and find the family hunting lodge," Sartre said. He felt that he was on to something now. He had probably thwarted their escape by ship and they were now fleeing over land. He only had to catch their trail now.

Jean could see it now. The road that turned off the main road and led down to the beach at Cape d'Antifer. The men and the wagon had been slowly paralleling the shore line for over an hour. Now, since they were at Cape d' Antifer where the ocean almost surrounded the point he could smell the salt air. He had always loved the smell of the salty ocean air and had learned to enjoy the smells and activities of the ocean as a boy when his father would bring him and Pierre to fish. His father, Dr. Jean Formy, Sr., loved to take his sons to the beach whenever he could get away from court activities and this was one of his favorite spots. Jean thought about old times but then forced his mind back to the task at hand.

"André!" Jean shouted as he turned to locate him. André's head snapped toward Jean and immediately spurred his horse to catch up to him. André came along side Jean. He did not speak but gave an inquiring look by slightly tilting his head and eyebrows up.

"André, we are going to turn off here and go down to the beach to unload. I want you and the rest of the men to go to the farm over there and give the animals and wagon to the farmer. After we unload, I will bring the horse and wagon to his farm. He is a friend of our family. You will have to tell the short story of what is going on and ask him to keep all the horses and wagons out of sight. If he gets questioned by authorities, tell him to say that we sold them to him at a bargain. Give him these gold pieces and ask him to try to get the horses back to my brother, if possible. Now be careful of his wife André. Try not to talk with her around. She is awfully shrewish."

Jean watched André and the other men ride toward the farm house for a few seconds and then looked at Jeanne, Louis, who were all looking at him. He took a deep breath, pointed his finger toward the road that led to the beach, and said, "Only two miles to the beach and freedom."

André's negotiation with the farmer had been easy. The man seemed to quickly grasp the situation and agreed to help. As André was finishing his conversation with the man, he noticed the wife walking up the road behind.

Good, André thought. *She didn't hear a thing but she*

probably did see the wagons on the road. He turned his horse from the farmer and tipped his hat to the wife and they started walking toward the beach to join the others.

The thunder of hooves from over a dozen soldiers on horseback always got everyone's attention. Sartre enjoyed the feeling of being at the head of such an expedition. They had been riding hard for an hour and were nearing the general area where he had seen two riders the day before. Some people at the garrison had known about the family hunting lodge and confirmed that it was in this area. It was time to stop and ask someone, and those seven or eight people working in the nearby field would do.

Sartre halted his detail in front of the people. They immediately stiffened and stood to face him.

"Where is the Formy lodge?" Sartre demanded.

One man pointed further down the road and said, "About one mile down the road and turn left. Go all the way to the end. It's the only house on the road."

Sartre resumed the hard pace down the road toward the lodge.

When the lodge came into view, Sartre knew he was too late. There was no activity, no people, no wagons, and no horses. They stormed into and around the lodge. There was no one and nothing to indicate their presence except someone had carved the word, "Montreal" into the top of a table.

One of the soldiers came in from the outside and said, "Sir, there are quite a few horse droppings out back near the stables. They are no more than a day old."

"Damn," Sartre spit out. "They probably left this morning. Quick, out to the road and head toward Cape d'Antifer. That's the only place they could have gone without our passing."

"It's a hour of hard riding sir," one of the soldiers said, "I hope the horses can take it."

"They'll have to," Sartre said. "If they don't, we confiscate more."

It was about three o'clock and Jeanne and Louis were playing in the water. "Jean, shouldn't the ship be here by now?"

"Yes," they should've been here by now."

"It's frightful, waiting like this", she said. Our very lives are in the hands of someone we hardly know."

Jean took out his telescope and looked at the seas. No sign of any ships, but there was a squall line moving in from the west. That would slow the ships if they could not see their navigation points. He removed the eyepiece and said with as much confidence as he could muster, "They should be here within the hour."

He looked at his family. To the casual passer-by they would appear to be on an outing at the beach, with mother and child playing at the water's edge, while the father munched on bread and cheese. The calmness of the scene certainly belied the turbulence of the situation.

"Jean," Jeanne called.

"Yes, *cheri*, what is it?"

"Isn't that cloud bank moving in awfully fast?"

Jean looked up from his bread and cheese and looked west. A wall of rain was on its way. By the looks of it, it was about fifteen minutes away.

Jeanne shouted, "Jean, look! There's the ship!"

Jean scanned the squall line for the ship with the telescope but could not locate it. He pulled the telescope down from his eye to see where Jeanne was pointing to. Then he saw it. It was rounding the point and was only two or three hundred yards off shore. He had been looking too far out. He raised the telescope back to his eye and located the ship and could make out some of the crew waving to them. They would be off shore and have a boat lowered in the water in a few minutes.

Jean turned and looked up the sandy road to see if the men were in sight and thought out loud, "Come on André, hurry up!"

André and the men were walking back from the farmer's house and were nearing the road that turned off to the beach. As they were about twenty yards down the beach road and about to lose sight of the main road, André took one last look down the road.

It was one of those times where an instant's recognition told the whole story. A dozen riders were coming hard down the road. André knew instinctively they were coming after them. There was something about the lead man that made André's stomach turn. He had seen the same man and horse before and he was sure it was Sartre.

"Oh God, run, they're coming!" André shouted.

The men didn't need any explanation, they knew by the sound and desperation in André's voice what was happening. They were all running for their lives.

Jean was pushing off the first of two row boats with Jeanne, Louis, and the luggage toward the ship. He turned to wade back to shore in the surf when he saw the men running down the road.

Sartre knew he was close. They had pushed hard and the horses were tired and lathered. He decided to stop at the next road that turned off to the beach and ask for information again and at the same time give the horses a break. He could see that a small road split off the main road a couple of hundred yards ahead, and decided to go to the farm on the right and see if they had seen anything. When he turned on the road to the farm they put all the horses at a walk. He could see a farmer working around the barn tending his horses and a woman working around the front of the house. As he neared the house, the woman took notice of them and turned to meet them.

"Madam, I am from the Citizen's Committee of LeHavre," he paused here. He loved to watch the reaction on people's faces when he told them he was from the powerful Citizen's Committee. "We are after a band of traitors trying to escape justice. It would be a wagon load of people and luggage along with men on horseback. Have you seen..."

"I saw them! I saw them!" she broke in excitedly and started pointing. "They went down the beach road just a few minutes ago."

Sartre and his men turned their horses and put them on a run down the lane to the road and then the sandy lane to the beach.

The old farmer walked out from the barn saw the situation and realized what his wife had done and uttered, "Oh *mon Dieu*."

When Sartre's men reached the road that turned off to the beach, the horses were slowed down by the sandiness of the road and their exhausted state. This infuriated him but he could do nothing but proceed at quarter speed.

Jean and the sailors were holding the second rowboat in the surf as André and the men came running up to the boat, winded.

"I saw them, riders, coming this way. I know it's Sartre," André said, trying to catch his breath.

86

Jean could do no more than nod and they all jumped in the boat and started rowing out to the ship. Even the sailors with them rowed hard, because even they did not want to deal with the Citizens Committee. They took the boat to the seaward side of the ship to mask as much of their loading activity as possible. As they were about to go behind the boat, Jean could see riders coming down the sandy road.

Jean and the men scrambled up the rope ladders and once aboard he raced to the other side of the ship and watched as Sartre and his men raced onto the beach.

The captain shouted for his sailors to make ready to sail. The men jumped into action as the wind picked up and the sails started to strain with the squall line closing in a few hundred feet away. The activity on the ship's deck was hectic with the sailors trying to hoist the last row boat and getting ready to make way for immediate sail.

Sartre rode to the water's edge and jumped off his horse. "Damn, damn, damn!" he shouted in a fit. He waved frantically at the ship to make it stay. "What ship is that?" he shouted to his men. No one answered because at that moment the squall line came across them, the boat, and the beach at the same time cutting visibility down to a couple hundred feet. His men were trying to grab hold of the reins of their horses so they could keep control of them.

Sartre dropped to his knees and cupped his hands over his eyes and peered at the ship. It looked a great deal like the *Le Bordeaux* but it was hard to make out. He could not move. He kneeled in the sand with the wind and rain blowing in his face and stared into the cloud bank for several minutes. Sartre stood up as the ship disappeared.

"It's not over yet Doctor Formy-Duval. It's not over!"

Charles Patton

"Interlude"

The trip to Los Palmays in the Canary Islands was a pleasant one for Jeanne. The weather was pleasant and the seas gentle. She spent most of her time on deck with little Louis who seemed to enjoy ship life, especially topside. Her favorite place to sit was on the steps leading to the ship's wheel. She turned herself sideways on the steps and put her back against the wall and her feet against the other side. The gentle rocking motion relaxed her and she began to doze. The sun was warm and had a soothing effect on her. It made the recent turmoil seem far away.

When she was not dozing she enjoyed watching Captain Chenier's men work the ship. The captain had a good crew which he acquired by being more generous than the average captain. He always had sailors asking to crew with him and as a result he picked the best.

Sometimes she would spend two or three hours topside watching the sailors climbing up and down the masts and do various duties around the ship. It took her mind off past and future problems. But eventually her mind would come back to their present situation and she would worry about Jean who was sleeping below. Since they had boarded the ship he had slept most of the time. He was exhausted by the drama that had been playing out for the last few weeks and once he reached a place where he felt safe he had collapsed in his hammock.

She watched Captain Chenier at the wheel of the ship. When an adjustment was needed on deck or with the sails

88

he would nod to a sailor or sometimes he only had to look at the problem. The sailors, who kept a close eye on their captain, would see what the problem was and adjust it. Jeanne felt safe with the captain's ship and crew. They were always well-mannered and treated her with respect.

"Captain Chenier?" Jeanne asked.

"*Oui, Madam,*" he answered.

"How many more days until Los Palmays?"

"Maybe four days if the good weather holds."

"And if it doesn't?"

"If we hit rough seas and bad winds, then maybe six or eight days."

Jeanne laid her head back against the stairwell and thought to herself about what the Canary Islands and Saint-Domingue would be like. She hoped that the good winds and gentle seas would continue. She held a drowsy Louis in her arms and both drifted into a light sleep.

Sartre fidgeted in his chair. The port master's office was an ill-kept space, stacked with papers and other seemingly useless paraphernalia, but his window commanded a view that covered all activity in the harbor. He had been waiting for more than an hour for the port master to return from a ship that he was inspecting.

It had taken over five hours to get back to the port of LeHavre and every hoof beat back seemed to pound humiliation and anger into Sartre. It was bad enough that the doctor had escaped, but to lose him by only a couple of minutes was pure frustration. Someone was coming up the stairs to the port master's office. Sartre broke away from his thoughts about the doctor, stood up, and straightened his coat.

"Well, look who's back," the port master said, as he walked through the door.

Sartre managed a superficial smile, nodded his head, and replied, "Oui, monsieur, I have come for information and your help once again."

"Sit down, please. Sit down and I'll see what I can do."

"Sir, it pains me to tell you this, but Doctor Formy-Duval has escaped me. I believe he met *LeBordeux* off the coast of Cape d'Antifer and boarded her there with all his compatriots."

"The scoundrel!" the port master said.

"I need information as to destinations of all ships that have left this harbor in the last twenty-four hours."

"Certainly sir, I have them written down here on the harbor log," the port master said as he fumbled through his papers on his desk to find the log book. "Ah, here it is. Now let me see, oh yes, six ships have left during the last day and night. Two are bound for Saint-Domingue, two for Africa, one for America, and one for Canada."

Sartre took interest at the mention of Canada as a destination and said, "What was the name of the Canadian bound ship?"

"Um..., yes it was *Le Bordeaux*, Captain Racine's vessel."

Sartre jumped up from the chair and said, "That's it! I thought it was *Le Bordeaux*. Is there another ship leaving for Canada soon?"

"Why yes, I just returned from the *Libertie*. She will make sail on the evening tide. I'm sure the Captain will make arrangements for a member of the Citizen's Committee if you wish to pursue your doctor."

The port master pointed out the *Libertie* for Sartre through the window and then added, "Remember all ships not going to other destinations in Europe almost always dock at the Canary Islands or Azores to top off their supplies and fresh water barrels. You might catch your doctor there if you are lucky."

"Yes, thank you, sir, thank you!" Sartre said, and ran down the stairs to find the *Libertie*.

Late in the afternoon on the fourth day out, Los Palmayes, a little harbor village in the Canary Islands, came into view. Jean and Jeanne heard the commotion up on deck when someone shouted, "Land, Los Palmays, off the port bow." Jean and Jeanne, with little Louis in her arms, came up on deck to watch their entrance into the harbor.

Captain Chenier looked down from the wheel and saw them come up on deck for the docking and smiled. He enjoyed having them on board ship. It was entertaining to have the doctor and his beautiful wife at the captain's table in the evenings. Good conversation was hard to come by on these long voyages and he would miss them after Los Palmays.

The Captain shouted down to them, "You might want to get a room at the inn tonight. Both the *L'Emanuel* and *Le Bordeaux* will probably sail on the afternoon tide tomorrow."

"Thanks Captain, I believe we'll do that," Jean shouted back.

"It will be your last chance at a steady bed and a decent meal for a few weeks." the Captain shouted.

Jeanne took in the harbor of Los Palmays as it came into view and thought to herself that it was little more than a small village with a harbor. Little fishing villages like this dotted the French coast every ten or fifteen miles at home. There would be little to do, but it would be nice to walk around the village and see what she could see and get all the exercise she could before she had to be cooped up on a ship for the next six to eight weeks.

A hundred miles behind, the *L"Emanuel* the *Libertie* was also closing in on Los Palmays. Sartre was up on the ship's deck with the Captain and a sailor at the wheel. Sartre was staring ahead and thinking that this was almost five full days he had been in pursuit of the doctor on this ship. He was wondering how close he was to his prey.

Sartre turned to the captain and asked, "Tell me, Captain, If a ship left LeHavre on the day after we did but on the following morning tide and both ships were heading to Los Palymas, how far back would that ship be?"

The captain shook his head and sucked in his breath and said, "It would be difficult to say for sure. The other ship might be faster or slower, heavier or lighter. It may have been luckier with the winds. It's hard to say for sure, but we could be as close as six hours behind or as far as twenty-four."

Sartre nodded his head. Desperation was starting to envelope him. He had been so close and now he may or may not be chasing the correct ship. He may or may not be closing in on the correct port.

Well, he thought to himself, *tomorrow will be the last play in this hand of human chance.* The game would not be over of course but he would have to re-evaluate his strategy if he did not find the doctor tomorrow. He walked to the rail of the ship, gripped it tightly, and stared out ahead of the ship.

Le Bordeaux was in the harbor and maneuvering for docking. Jeanne and Louis were watching the sailors scramble about the decks and rigging when she noticed that Jean had gone to the seaward side of the ship and was leaning on the rail looking out to sea.

"Jean, will you stop torturing yourself. Once we get on

the ship tomorrow, it will be all over. It's practically over now. Let's relax and enjoy the evening. All right?"

"I guess you are right. There must be a tavern here, with all the sailors around. Let's see if we can put some life in this little town tonight."

Jeanne awoke before Jean the next morning. She sat on the side of the bed and stretched and then started smiling when she remembered the night before at the tavern where Jean had taken them to eat. They both had too much wine which had made her head swim. They had laughed and enjoyed listening to the local singers and their instruments. Little Louis had looked in amazement at his parents laughing so much. When they returned to their room Louis was already asleep in Jean's arms, and they put him down in a small side bed. Jeanne smiled again while reliving their lovemaking. She looked over at Jean and said, "Wake up, you rogue. You had too good of a time last night."

"What?" Jean said, half sitting up and holding one hand over his eyes. "What did I do?"

"Well, you ravaged me, when you got me back here to this room", she said with a false primness. "I hope the people in the next room were sound asleep or they might have thought you were hurting me."

"You mean with all that screaming and biting you did?"

Jeanne ignored him for a few seconds while she put her hat and shawl on and picked up Louis. She walked to the dresser with the bowl of water on it, turned to him and said with all the virtue she could muster, "I do not scream or bite."

Jean groaned and fell back on the bed and whispered, "Oh yes you do, princess. Oh yes you do."

Charles Patton

Jeanne spent the morning going to every shop and walking up and down every street in the small town while Jean stayed in the harbor to make sure that their goods were transferred from *Le Bordeaux* to the *L'Emanuel*, which had arrived during the night. As soon as the transfer was complete *Le Bordeaux* pulled out early for Canada.

Jean was standing in the doorway of the hatch going down into *L'Emanuel*, when he noticed another ship slipping into the harbor. The *Libertie* was the name and Jean's apprehensions arose in him again. He didn't know why, but he decided to crouch in the doorway and watch this ship. Jean saw several men at the wheel and could discern nothing unusual until one man walked to the side of the ship and started taking note of all the ships in the harbor. It was Sartre.

Jean ran down into the ship to find Captain Racine who was overseeing the placement of some last minute cargo.

"Racine, I just saw Sartre arrive on a ship coming into the harbor."

Captain Racine froze for a moment and asked, "Are you sure?"

"Yes, yes, I'm positive."

"Where is your wife?" the Captain asked, almost in a whisper.

"She's in town, shopping," Jean said.

"I'll go find her, stay below, out of sight." The Captain turned to his first mate and said, "Be ready for immediate departure as soon as I return with the doctor's wife."

Sartre started inquiries about *Le Bordeaux* as soon as he walked off the ship. Jean watched him through a porthole as Sartre questioned several people on the docks. It was obvious that he was distressed about missing *Le Bordeaux* and at one point threw his hat on the ground. One good thing, Jean thought, *Sartre has bought the Canada story for our destination.*

Sartre stormed off the docks and headed up the street toward the port master's office with his head down, talking to himself. As he did, he almost ran over Jeanne and Louis.

"Pardon, Madam", Sartre uttered and hurried on.

Captain Racine watched the whole scene with his heart pounding and his knees feeling weak.

"Madam, madam," Captain Racine said in a forced but low voice, "That was Sartre who almost ran over you. He just arrived on the *Libertie.*"

"Oh, mon Dieu, do you think he recognized me?" Jeanne asked in horror.

"No, you wouldn't be standing here now if he did. Come on, we're departing as soon as we get back to the ship."

Sartre was in the port master's office getting all the information he could about *Le Bordeaux.* He asked questions about and gave descriptions of Dr. Formy-Duval.

"No, no, I have not seen anyone like that, I'm sorry," exclaimed the port master.

Sartre collapsed in a chair. He was bitterly disappointed at such a close call.

"That's strange," the port master said looking out the window, "*L'Emanuel* is leaving early," and noted it in his log book.

Sartre took no notice of the comment. He was planning his trip to Canada to continue the search for Dr. Jean Formy-Duval.

Charles Patton

Centaur of the Savannahs

Beside the ungathered rice he lay, His sickle in his hand:
His breast was bare, his matted hair was buried in the sand.
Again, in the mist and shadow of sleep, He saw his Native Land.
<u>*The Slaves Dream*</u>
Henry Wadsworth Longfellow

Book Two

The Centaur of the Savannas

The Chosen one

Pierre Baptiste sat at the window of his cottage looking out over the nearby mountains and watched the varying shades of another colorful Caribbean sunset. He was ninety-five years old now but never tired of watching the sunsets from the heights of the Bréda plantation near Cap Francais in San Domingue. It was late Sunday afternoon, his favorite day and his favorite time of the day. He closed his eyes and soaked in the feeling of natural beauty and family unity. He, his wife, and children always spent Sunday going to church and then used the rest of the day in the cottage as a day of rest interspersed with family talk, religious discussion, and prayer. He felt he had been lucky in his life. Many good things had always followed the bad ones. As a small boy in Africa he had been captured and sold to the slave traders. He had survived the long voyage across the ocean and then the seasoning process. This process normally happened during the first year on the island which put each person, slave or colonist, through the ravages of malaria, yellow fever, and other assorted

97

diseases. Only one out of every two slaves survived both ordeals.

Somehow he was lucky enough to become a slave of Jesuit priests on the island. They put him through their school and taught him to read and write in French along with a fair knowledge of Latin, but the most useful thing they taught him was nature and how to use it. They taught him how to make and brew curative potions from plants for both man and animals. This had been his trade in life along with his other plantation duties.

The black population held him as a type of voodoo priest with special knowledge, and he was looked upon with respect and awe. He had tried to disassociate himself from the voodoo religion through his whole life because he was a devout Catholic and believed without doubt in the Christian way. When the Jesuits had been forced off of the island several decades ago they had released their slaves, and he had found work as a "freedman" on the Bréda plantation. They had provided him a cottage and a small plot of land for him to tend on a share system with the plantation.

He had picked where he worked with care and felt lucky to be on the Bréda plantation. It was only one of about a half dozen plantations on the island where the owners had specifically instructed the overseers to be lenient to the slaves even if it affected the production of the crops.

Thousands of other plantations on the island were run from a standpoint of pure greed. Most of the owners and overseers were there to make as quick a fortune as possible and then return to France. This made them work the slaves at a merciless pace. Slaves were required to work from sunrise to sunset six days a week and tend to their own garden on Sunday. As a result they never had enough to eat and roamed the countryside at night trying to steal food from other gardens. During the day they were pushed to the point of exhaustion. The only exceptions to this were the house slaves.

The slave population could not sustain itself through re-population because of the high death rate due to yellow fever, malnutrition and the fact that the female bodies were so stressed by the boat trip from Africa that once they reached Saint-Domingue it took two years before they could become fertile again. This combination of factors created a demand for a lucrative slave trade.

Although Pierre Baptiste was not a slave, his wife was. Therefore his children were born as slaves. He would have liked to have bought his children out of slavery, but was always giving his meager savings to those who needed it more. He had longed for his family's freedom but was not bitter over it. He realized through watching other tortured minds that if a man will let it, bitterness and anger would eat away at him until no one could stand to be around him, even the ones who loved him. Pierre took some solace in the Bible and how it taught one to do their best at whatever you do even if you were a slave, but he knew that someday, just like Moses and the Pharaohs, a time was coming when God would raise up someone and the consequences would be bloody for the people on this island.

Francis Dominique Toussaint Baptiste was Pierre Baptiste's son and he was watching his father rest. This was one of those times when he could never tell if his father was sleeping or possibly communicating with God. So great was their respect for the old man that whenever he was in one of these spells they became very quiet for fear of disturbing a possible conversation with the Almighty.

Pierre opened his eyes and saw Toussaint looking at him. He had hoped that maybe his son would seek freedom and help in his people's deliverance. He had taught him how to read and write French along with a few Latin phrases. He had also taught him all he knew about plant lore and how to make medicine. But his son was 47 now and probably too old to participate in any revolutionary struggle. His son would have been a fine leader. He had natural leadership qualities. People came from all over to talk over matters with him or have him put together a cure for some sick person or animal.

As a young man he had a natural thirst for knowledge and books. The owners of the plantation and the local priest gave him all the books that were available and he devoured them. He was also a good athletic and a natural horseman. So great was his horsemanship that the local priest had given him the nickname, the Centaur of the Savannas.

"Father, I thought you were asleep," Toussaint said.

A slow smile came across his face. "No, I was thinking back to when you were a young man and people would come from all over on Sunday afternoons just to watch you ride and jump Monsieur de Libertat's horses over the fences."

"That was a long time ago and they don't come around anymore", Toussaint said, smiling back.

"No, who was that who came to talk to you last night?"

"I thought you were asleep; besides he only wanted a cure for an animal."

"Oh, really? Don't try to fool your old father. I know who that was and what he wanted. It was political, wasn't it?"

Toussaint paused for a few seconds. He should have known that his father would know. He didn't realize that he had seen the man.

"Yes, father, it was political."

"What did he want?"

He had never concealed anything from his father and he wasn't going to start now. "Boukman is organizing a revolt and he is trying to establish contacts with leaders in every district."

"I know about Boukman. He's from Jamaica and a runaway slave. He's a dangerous man, so be careful. What did he want from you?"

"They're planning a revolt. It's still in the beginning stages but they want me to organize this area and become a district leader when it comes."

His father leaned back and thought about this for a while and then spoke, "If a revolt comes, it will probably be violent at first. The leaders will be hunted down and killed while the whites are strong, but if the struggle continues then the whites will not be able to withstand a long war. There are ten times more blacks on the island than whites. You should see what happens and if it looks like a true revolution, then get in there for the long haul."

"Don't worry, Father. I'll take care of myself," Toussaint said. He knew that while his father wanted him to be a leader in the rebellion, he did not want to see his son die either.

He had already committed himself to help in the struggle for reforms, which he felt was the right path instead of a bloody revolution. The problem was trying to convince Boukman and his followers of that path. They wanted his participation for months because of his influence. They knew he had been given *liberte de*

101

savanne, which granted him all the rights of a freedman while legally under the protection of his owner. This gave him unlimited travel opportunities and afforded him the opportunity to organize and act as a courier. He had agreed to help but only as a courier and organizer. He did not want to become involved in the command structure until he better understood their intent.

Toussaint was cautious in all he did. Even in his private life he was careful. As a young man he had been offered many exotic and sultry mistresses for a wife from the surrounding area but he had somehow managed to delay and hold off from these offers. He had wanted to choose his own woman and at age forty did so from a relative of his father's first wife. He had chosen Suzanne Simon who was five years his junior. She was plump and already had a four-year-old son from a mulatto of previous acquaintance.

The fact that Toussaint was happy with Suzanne was evident in the later writings about his life where he wrote, *"We went to labor in the field, my wife and I, hand in hand. Scarcely were we conscious of the fatigue of the day. Heaven always blessed our toil. Not only did we swim in abundance, but we had the pleasure of giving food to Blacks who needed it. On the Sabbath and on festival days we went to church—my wife, my parents and myself. Returning to our cottage, after a pleasant meal, we passed the remainder of the day in the family circle, and we closed it by prayer, in which all took part.*

This was the peaceful setting from which he started moving away when he was nearing the age of fifty. A drastic change was coming, and whether he liked it or not, he was to be the leading figure in it.

Saint-Domingue (Haiti)

"The Pearl of the Antilles"

L'Emanuel slipped into the outer edge of the harbor in Cap Francais two hours before midnight. Jean and Jeanne watched as it was anchored on the edge of the harbor. Dozens of merchant ships competed for space in the harbor. Half of them were from France and the rest were from the United Sates. The city, for all its impact and fame in Europe, was actually a small to medium sized port with a couple of hundred houses and buildings, but its surroundings were stunning.

The city lay at the foot of a mountain that spread up like an amphitheater displaying all of its majestic greenery and foliage. Now, as full darkness settled, the city sparkled at its base and the lights of the houses faded as the eye moved up the mountain.

Captain Racine was finishing the anchoring process with the crew when he saw his passengers looking at the city. He walked over to them and said, "Well there she is, the richest export harbor in the western world. This one little island supplies almost all the sugar, coffee, and indigo for all of Europe. Most of it comes out of this port and the rest out of Port-au-Prince."

"Why are so many American ships here? I thought colonies could trade with no one except their mother country," Jeanne asked.

"That's supposed to be true. That one law causes more trouble with the planters than anything else. The Americans are here because they are much closer than Europe and there is friendship left over from the American Revolution between the Americans and French. Remember, the French helped the Americans defeat the British at the end of their war.

"The local government turns its head and allows the trade to happen. Legally, the Americans are not supposed to be here but the planters can sell to them at their crops' real value, not the sixty percent reduction in price that is required of them, by law, when they sell to the brokers in France. So, there is a great deal of winking at the law here for the Americans."

Jeanne turned to Jean and asked, "Can we sell our sugar to the Americans?"

"We already do. Our plantation is near Port-au-Prince. The local government is very understanding. We sell almost our entire crop to the Americans."

Jeanne smiled and said, "We must do well then?"

Jean smiled back and said, "When our family obtained the land grant from the King about ten years ago we sent one of our overseers from the estate in France to start it up. During the last five years it has virtually guaranteed that our family coffers will stay full."

"How do we get to Port-Au-Prince?" Jeanne asked.

"We'll have to find a ship here in Cap Francais that's making other stops around the island and book passage."

"Don't worry madam," Captain Racine said. "There're plenty of boats going to Port-Au-Prince. You'll be there in a few days."

Jeanne thought about this for a moment and said, "Not only are we away from a civilized culture in France but we are going to be away from any culture at all on this island by being so far from Cap Francais."

"That may not be so bad," Jean said. "We will be away from the revolutionary problems that plague the Northern Plain and I'm not sure I would want to have my family around Cap Francais."

"Why is that?" Jeanne asked.

"Well, they say that the two wickedest cities since Sodom and Gomorrah are Port Royal in Jamaica and Cap Francais."

"Aye, that's right, madam," Captain Racine piped in. "My sailors are getting a row boat ready to go into town now. They don't plan to miss a night."

"Hey, isn't that André getting in the rowboat too?" Jeanne said.

"Yes madam, one of them mulatto ladies is going to get him for sure tonight," the captain said with a big smile on his face.

"Well I sure hope your other friends behave. I'll have to keep an eye on them for their wives," Jeanne said.

"Yeah, I know they'll really appreciate it," Jean said. "Come on, Princess, let's go to bed and leave the town and the ladies to the sailors."

Jean awoke early the next morning. He put on his clothes, trying not to wake Jeanne or Louis, and went on deck. Victor, Romaine, Jacques, and André were sitting near the bow watching the sunrise. They were feeling the same fears that he was feeling. They were all anxious about their fates and what the future would bring to them and their families.

The smell of fresh coffee wafted past him. He had not tasted coffee since France. One of the sailors must have brought some coffee beans back from shore last night. He poured himself a mug and sat on the ship's rail near them.

"Morning, Jean," Victor said.

"Good morning," Jean said and raised his cup to toast them.

Jean leaned back against some of the ship's rigging and watched the reflection of the sunrise off the water between the ship and the harbor. No one said anything. They sat quietly, sipped their coffee, and watched the sunrise until the colors were gone.

A conversation started about the town in front of them. They covered everything from business opportunities to the pleasures of the town. The old topic of their immediate future came up again and Jean took the opportunity and said to Victor, Romain, Jacques, and André, "I know you are not sure what to do with yourselves and your families for the next few weeks or at least until you can get your future endeavors started. Well, Jeanne and I would like to invite any and all of you to stay at our family plantation near Port-Au-Prince until you are ready to leave."

They were all pondering Jean's offer when Victor said, "Jean, I have something a little different planned. There is something about this island that troubles me. I can't quite put my finger on it, but it unsettles me." He paused for a moment and then continued. "I'm going to go on to New Orleans in Louisiana."

"Are you sure Victor", Romaine said. "That's awfully close to the English."

"Well, they are not English. They're Americans and they fought the English too, so I don't think they will be so bad to live near," Victor said. "So what are you going to do, Romaine?"

"I think I will stay here with an uncle in Cap Francais and get into a trading business right here in the harbor," Romaine said.

"You think you can start up a business with the snap of your fingers?" Jacques said.

"Start? No. Buy? Yes. Captain Racine says he knows of several successful businesses here in the harbor where the owners are eager to sell and get back to France," Romaine said.

"Good, good," said Jacques. "You can buy sugar from my plantation and make me rich."

They all laughed and then Jean turned to André and said, "And you André?"

"Jean, I appreciate your offer to help me get started while I stay at your plantation but I think that I will go to New Orleans with Victor," André said.

Jean had thought André would have stayed with him but Jean smiled his agreement, raised his coffee mug and toasted, "To our future and good fortunes." All raised their mugs and drank to it.

Jean heard a scuffle of footsteps running up the ladder and saw Jeanne run to the far rail and throw up over the side.

"I don't know what's wrong with Jeanne. She's been sick for the past three or four mornings." But as a doctor he had a sneaking suspicion of what was the matter.

Port-Au-Prince was another disappointment for Jeanne. The buildings were small, the roads narrow and dirty, and even the port buildings looked small and hot. She had thought Cap Francais looked destitute, but this was miserable. The small schooner they had booked passage on was siding up to the wharf and all hands were busy securing the boat.

"Don't judge it too harshly yet," Jean said.

"I know. I'm trying not to. I have to keep telling myself

that if we had stayed in France that we would probably have been found out and executed by now, although I'm not sure if this isn't a fate worse than death." Jeanne said.

"*Mon cher*," Jean said, "Wait until you see the plantation. My family has spent a great deal of money on the construction of the house and its furnishings. I have been assured that it is a beautiful and comfortable estate. You have always preferred country life to city life, even in France. We may not have all the elegance of France but think of the good things we will have here; fresh fruit growing all year around. Not only for the rich but for anyone who wants to pick it off the tree. Remember how you huddled around the fireplace in France for seven or eight months a year? Here, in Saint-Domingue, they don't even use fireplaces except to cook."

"What about friends? Will we have someone to talk to?"

"Of course, the province we live in is filled with plantations owned by other members of the Formy family, also there are several plantations owned by the Crousilleaus, my older brother's wife's family. You know that."

Jeanne picked up Louis and put his feet on the boat's railing, held him with one arm, and pointed out things on the shore to him while Jean made arrangements to get their trunks off the ship and onto a wagon. She couldn't help but think about the things that Jean had pointed out. She hated winter time in Europe. The winters were miserable, the houses drafty, and you couldn't take a bath for months, just sponge off as best as you could. Only the strongest of children made it through the tough winters and sicknesses. Oh yes, the fruit! In France only the rich could afford it, and then only if they had connections with someone at one of the ports. In Cap Francais, Jean had given her a whole basket of fruit from the local market. She had never had so much fresh fruit before. She and Louis had eaten the whole basket in one afternoon. Living in St. Domingue might be a pleasant experience, but she would miss France and the cultural atmosphere.

"Come on, Jeanne, grab Louis and get in the wagon. The driver says we have enough daylight left to get to the plantation at Pays Pourri," Jean shouted from the dock.

"Does he know where the plantation is?" she asked.

The driver interrupted, "Oui, madam. Everyone knows Pays Pourri, and the Crousilleau and Formy plantations. It's in the Croix des Bouquets area. People don't call it Pays Pourri though. They mostly call it Crousilleau. The slaves just call it *Crus-au.*"

"Why does everyone know about the Formy and Crousilleau plantations?," she asked Jean after getting into the wagon.

"I think it's because they take up so much land area. When our family received the land grant from the King, it was settled by four of the Formy and Crousilleau family members. The boundaries were one big square. So the four families divided it into four properties. Then the families built the plantation houses where the four properties joined. All the houses are within sight of each other. By being so close they share resources, slaves and pool their crops to leverage the best price. They also meet and talk almost every evening to discuss the day's events, plan strategy, and socialize."

Jean kept up a steady stream of conversation as she gazed at the countryside. Flowers covered the countryside. She had never imagined flowers like this. The tropical flowers were much more vivid in color when compared to European flowers. The varied colors of reds, oranges, and purples led a visual assault on her senses.

Every few miles they would pass plantations that were beautiful country estates patterned after French country homes, but with a more open and casual design. There was always plenty of activity with slaves tending houses, gardens, and many field activities.

She was entertaining the fact that she might enjoy it here when their wagon came around the corner of a field where some slaves were cutting sugar cane with their machetes. There was a dozen of them and were accompanied by a white field boss on a horse. He had a large whip draped over his saddle. The field boss raised the coiled whip to the brim of his hat and tipped it as a passing salute. They waved and smiled back at him, but then Jeanne met the stare of two or three of the slaves. She had never seen such eyes of contempt. It worried her to know that these were the people they made their fortunes off of and they were always only a few yards away. Captain Racine had said there were ten blacks to every one white in St. Domingue.

One slave stopped, straightened, and stared at them. Immediately a whip cracked as it struck his back. The slave recoiled from the strike but didn't utter a word. He gave them one last look of contempt and continued with his task.

Belle walked through the plantation house. She ran it with authority and tact. She managed the Formy house the way she wanted it to run and didn't tolerate sloppy work. She was a slave herself, but authority had been granted to her. She had the authority to banish slaves from the house and put them back in the fields. She walked from room to room, servant to servant, leveling small criticisms mixed with tiny drops of praise. That was her technique. Tell them where improvement was needed, but end it on a word of praise. This was her late afternoon check to see if the day's duties had been accomplished. Most of the servants could now return to their quarters except for the ones who were preparing and serving supper. The kitchen staff stiffened a little as they heard her footsteps coming.

"Louise, you know I like to have two extra places, not one, set at the table," Belle said.

"*Oui*," Louise said and hurried off to correct her mistake.

"Zoé, do you have the fruit dish ready?"

"*Oui*, mother, I have cut all the fruits into fancy little shapes and arranged them just so."

Belle eyed the fruit platter with suspicion. It was beautifully done but she gave out only a grunt of approval. She was tougher on her daughter than anyone else. She did not want to show any favoritism to her daughter in front of the other staff. Belle expected a great deal from her people and she got it, especially from her daughter. Zoé knew from the time she could first understand and talk that her mother expected her to do her best, no exceptions.

"Mother," Zoé asked, "why are we preparing such a large dinner tonight? Is there going to be anyone else besides Master Jacques? Do you think the new masters are coming tonight?"

"I don't know child; I just have a feeling that we need to do something extra."

This set the whole staff off on the same conversation that had been raging every night for a couple of weeks, ever since they had gotten word that the young Dr. Formy-Duval, his wife, and child were to arrive soon.

Belle leaned against the door frame, looked out down the road, and thought back to when the young doctor's father had been there ten years earlier to help set up the plantation. Doctor Formy had been the real leader among all his cousins when they were laying out the plantations and trying to clear fields for their first crops.

The doctor had noticed Belle's ability to organize and get results when she had produced a garden that yielded enough food for all, owners and slaves. Things had been better back then but it slowly deteriorated when he went back to France and left his cousins and Master Marc to run his plantation. The plantation did all right, but the slaves did not. All they seemed interested in was profit and replacing the slaves they had worked to death. The only reason that she, Jules, and Zoé were alive after ten years was because she was able to work in the house and garden. Jules was her man, her mate.

As a slave, Jules' first destination had been French Guiana and clearing land. Two long, miserable years later he was re-sold and ended up in Saint-Domingue. By the time he reached the Crousilleau Plantation he was a beaten man; figuratively and literally, but Belle took notice of him, and under her care she brought him back; body and soul.

They were not allowed to marry. Didn't matter though, she knew they were married in God's sight. Jules was the one who had told her what to do each night during the first year she had the garden. He could do anything with plants. He seemed to have a magical touch with anything he worked on or planted. He loved to make things grow.

Zoé watched her mother as she rested against the door frame. She looked tired. She was half listening to the kitchen chatter and half looking at something outside. Almost imperceptibly Belle shifted positions and her eyes narrowed.

"What is it, mother?" Zoé asked.

"They're here. If I'm not mistaken that is the young

doctor and his family coming up the road now. Louise, set up the whole table for company," Belle said, then rattled off a whole set of new orders.

Zoé took a deep breath. The masters represented a fear-fascination syndrome with her. She had heard of new masters moving in and being cruel. Many had died on other plantations, but she had heard of a few rare cases where conditions improved, because the master was kind of heart. Zoé had tried to get her mother to tell her what she thought would happen when the new masters arrived, but Belle would not say. She wanted her to say that things would be better because the young doctor's father was a good man. Zoé knew her mother felt it might get better, but she never expressed her thoughts except to say, "We'll see."

Jean looked over the plantation and the house as the wagon made its way up to the house. He could tell almost to the instant when they were recognized. The people inside the house and out could be seen in an explosion of activity. Runners had been sent to the other Formy plantations, doors and windows had been flung open, people were looking and pointing. Even the dogs picked up the excitement. They started barking at the wagon as it approached the house.

Belle walked out to welcome the new family. She knew that Master Marc, the overseer, was still in the fields with the workers and it fell on her to welcome any guests. As the wagon rolled to a stop, she said, "Welcome to the Crousilleau plantation, Monsieur Formy-Duval."

"Belle?" Jean asked.

"*Oui*, Monsieur?"

"I guessed so; my father talked about you many times. I am so glad to finally meet you."

"Is your father well?"

"Yes, considering that I have greatly worried him in the last few months," Jean said with a smile.

Belle's heart jumped; she knew that smile. It was just like his father's. In only a few moments of conversation, she had judged that he was much like his father and conditions would not get worse.

"Oh, Belle, this is my wife, Jeanne, and our son, Louis," he said.

"Hello, Belle, you don't know how glad we are to finally be here," Jeanne said. "Louis, say hello to Belle."

Louis smiled shyly and hid his face behind his mother's skirt.

"Please, come in the house. We have supper ready." Belle said. "I will have someone take your trunks inside."

Out of the corner of his eye Jean saw that a horseman was coming fast. *That must be Marc*, he thought.

"Monsieur Formy-Duval, I'm Marc, the overseer of your lands," he said. He then, with hat in hand, gave a sweeping arc of his hat and a slight bow from the waist.

"Marc, the man who captains our holdings here in Saint-Domingue. My father sends his regards," Jean replied.

"Thank you, Monsieur Formy-Duval. Your father and I started this together. It has been a slow process, but I have become very proud of it."

"And so you should be. It looks beautiful and is, as always, most profitable."

"Thank you Monsieur, but I must leave you. I have to finish closing down the day's work. I will return later to chat with you. Belle will take good care of all your needs."

"Yes, by all means, do what has to be done".

Marc nodded his head in a slight curtsey and charged back to the fields.

"Follow me," Belle said. She was anxious to get them

into the house where she could proceed with getting them settled and fed.

Belle had hardly gotten the trunks to their rooms before other family members in the area started arriving, all carrying food. Soon an impromptu feast and party was under way. This lasted until about eleven o'clock. It would have lasted longer, but they were considerate of the new arrivals' long and tiring trip. Jean and Jeanne bid their last guest *adieu* and fell, exhausted, into bed.

Belle and Zoé entered the door of their cabin, trying not to wake Jules, but he was sitting up in bed with his back propped against the wall and was looking out the window.

"What are you doing up? You know that whip cracks at dawn," Belle scolded Jules as she lit a candle.

"I know, but I couldn't sleep until you told me about the new master. What are they like?" Jules asked, turning his head to stare out the window. He didn't want to seem like he was too anxious or scared.

Belle knew exactly what he was feeling. Life was hard in the fields. Even if a field slave was treated with some measure of consideration he could only expect to live ten years. Only a slight difference in treatment by the owners, good or bad, could make dramatic differences in a slave's health and longevity. She looked at his exposed chest. She remembered when they were first living together how muscular his chest had been. Now, long days and minimal nourishment had brought his build down to a slim and wiry frame. He would not have lasted this long had she not worked in the kitchen and could sneak food home for him. She walked over and crawled on the bed with him and put her arms around him and laid her head on the back of his shoulder.

"Don't worry, husband," she said. "He's like his father.

There's a goodness in him. I can see it in the gentle words he uses when he talks to his little boy and there is a kindness of touch and a look of love for his wife whenever he is near her." She could feel her husband choke, ever so slightly, with emotion.

"That's good," he said after a long pause, "that he's like his father. I didn't know him except to see him ride through the fields occasionally. But, it could be bad, too. He might be too nice and not stand up to the overseers," He continued to look out the window at the rising moon.

Belle knew he could be right and she didn't want to give him any false hopes of life being any better. Life had enough disappointments.

"Well, at least it shouldn't get any worse. Try not to worry," Belle said.

Zoé spoke from where she was sitting on her bed across the room, "Daddy, they are real nice and he has all sorts of new plans for the plantation."

Jules heart sunk at that bit of news. It usually meant clearing more land, the hardest work of all.

"I heard him tell his uncle that he wanted to start a new type of garden and try to raise his own seed. He also wants to raise special plants to make into medicines," Zoé said.

"I didn't hear that Zoé. When did he say that?" Belle asked.

"When I was serving wine to the men in the parlor. He's just full of ideas. Sort of set his uncles back a bit. I could tell they's not too sure about it."

Jules turned his head toward Zoé and listened to her rattle on. He would give anything to work with the new garden. He loved making things come to life. He also loved to watch and listen to Zoé talk. Belle's love kept him alive, but Zoé's doings kept him interested in life. Zoé had been eight years old when he and Belle started living together.

He and Zoé had bonded during his first year with Belle and Zoé quickly adopted him as a father figure. She loved the attention he gave her.

Zoé was a product of Belle's affair on another plantation with the owner's son. It had been an affair of necessity for Belle; done to get extra food and better treatment for her mother. It worked for a while, but the family became uncomfortable, having Belle and her child around, so they sold them to the Formy plantation. It didn't matter to Jules though. He didn't know how he could have loved her any more than he did. Zoé had turned into a beautiful mulatto woman and she thought of him as her father.

Belle had worked hard to disguise her daughter's beauty. She made her wear loose, colorless clothes and she always had her wear a scarf to hide her hair which, with only a little effort, could be straightened. She did not want Zoé to be taken to a brothel in Port-Au-Prince or worse, up to Cap Francais. Many mulatto women married well by doing so, but Belle was not going to have her daughter prostitute herself for anybody or anything like she had to do when she was young.

"...And he said that he was going to pick out a place for that test garden tomorrow..."

Belle's head jumped when Zoé said that. She needed to get to the young doctor first thing tomorrow to get Jules's name in for the new garden. She had to. Jules couldn't make it through many more seasons.

Jeanne walked through the dining room and into the kitchen. She had Louis in tow by the hand and he ready for breakfast. She stopped in amazement. Tray after tray of prepared fruits and pastries were on platters everywhere for breakfast.

117

"Belle!" Jeanne exclaimed.

The kitchen staff became silent.

"*Oui, Madam,*" Belle answered. She had the doctor figured out but she wasn't sure about the wife.

"Are we having company for breakfast? All this couldn't possibly be for us," Jeanne said not believing what she was seeing.

"*Oui Madam*, it is for you and your little boy," Belle said.

Jeanne laughed and said, "Belle, you don't have to do this for us. We don't eat that much in the mornings." Jeanne put her hand to her forehead, laughed, and exclaimed again, "*Mon Dieu*! Look at all this food. Belle, we must talk about the menus when we finish our breakfast."

Belle relaxed along with the rest of the staff. At least she had a good humor about her. She may not have been hungry but little Louis looked like he was mighty interested in those pastries.

Jean walked in the back door of the kitchen and caught the look of amazement in Jeanne's eye, sized up the situation and said, "What's the matter Jeanne; aren't you hungry?"

Jeanne couldn't say anything else; she stood there shaking her head, holding the tips of her fingers over her lips.

Jean grasped Louis by the hand and hustled him toward the dining room table. He looked at Belle as he walked past her and said in a whisper, "It looks wonderful Belle; bring it on."

As they were seating themselves at the table Jeanne said, "Jean, even the King and Queen of France don't have food like this and most of it will be wasted."

"Don't worry about it, Princess. I'm sure they wanted to

impress you this morning and they just overdid it a bit. Besides, many of the planters here on the island expect to be treated like royalty. This is nothing unusual on most plantations. If you don't like it they will make whatever you tell them to prepare. Remember, this isn't only for us, the house servants will eat off this all morning."

Jean pointed at Louis. His face was covered with the remnants of fruits, juices and a big smile. "I think we've found a mango lover here." Jean said.

Jeanne grabbed a napkin and started wiping Louis's face.

"I'm a mango lover, Mommy," Louis said, mimicking his father.

In the kitchen Zoé asked Belle, "Is everything all right, Mamma?"

"I think so. I don't think Madam Jeanne likes to have too big a fuss made over her."

Zoé laughed, "That would be a big difference from them other plantation wives."

"Yeah, I believe she is different," Belle said. She was trying to think of a way to talk to the doctor about her Jules and the test garden. That is where the doctor had been since early sunrise, walking around the area near the house and barns.

Belle was deep in thought when Jean walked out of the house to begin his first day of inspecting the plantation. She pulled her thoughts together and followed him out the back door.

"Dr. Formy-Duval," Belle tried to catch his attention.

Jean had signaled for his horse when he heard Belle call his name. He turned and saw Belle clutching at her skirts trying to catch up to him. "Belle, Dr. Formy-Duval is a mouthful to say, why don't you call me Dr. Jean."

This caught Belle off guard. It was not what she had on

119

her mind and it sounded too familiar, especially if other white people were around. She thought about it for a second and said, "You don't think that will get me in trouble, do you? We're not supposed to call white people by their first names."

"If it makes you uncomfortable then call me Dr. Formy-Duval when other white people are around. Otherwise, call me Dr. Jean."

Belle took a deep breath and said, "*Oui*, Dr. Jean, I wanted to ask you about your new garden."

This surprised Jean and he said, "Belle how do you know about my test garden?"

"Zoé heard you tell your family about it last night. Anyway I wanted to tell you about someone who can make anything grow. He loves to garden and he experiments with plants."

"Really, how does he experiment with plants?"

"He can cut a branch off one tree and tie it into another fruit tree with a string and make a mango grow on another tree. Sometimes it tastes like a mango and sometimes it tastes like both."

Jean couldn't believe his good fortune. Someone right here on Crousilleau who could graft plants. "Who is this person?"

"It's my man, Jules. He works in the fields for you. He'd just be wasting away out there in the hot sun when he could be helping you in that new garden."

One of the servants placed his horse's reins in his hands. "Thank you, Belle." He mounted the horse and thought about it for a second and said, "I'll have to ask Master Marc his opinion about the matter."

"That's all right. He's a hard worker. Master Marc knows Jules," Belle shouted trying to contain her excitement.

Jean spent the rest of the morning with Marc. They rode over every inch of the plantation and visited the other family plantations that were nearby. Jean knew a great deal about farming. His father raised him on their estate in the country, living in the city as little as possible. His father's passion was growing medicinal herbs and plants. They scoured the woods and coastal plains looking for known medicinal plants and experimenting with new ones. They had their own herb and medicinal garden filled with unusual plants. This knowledge of plants worked its way to all the other farm activities, especially the cash crops which was the main farm activity.

A farmer with large land holdings and farm crops could make a great deal more money than a doctor. The most lucrative operation of all was to have a plantation in the Caribbean where sugar, coffee, or spices could be sent back to France. Vast fortunes could and were made in only a few short years, many, many times over what a doctor could make.

Marc was impressed by his knowledge of farming but he wasn't surprised. His father had been the same way. His same penetrating line of questions was just like his father's.

"Marc, what's your theory on treatment of slaves?"

"Well, there are two theories. The first one is to treat them hard, feed them only enough to get by on, and work them to death in about four to five years. The second is the one I subscribe to. Don't use the whip except when necessary, give them a minimal amount to eat, give them one shirt and one pair of pants. Even then you have to replace them every eight to ten years."

Jean listened. He knew he was going to change a few things but not on his first day. Each family had their own

121

slaves but many times they combined their slave force, a type of cooperative, where slaves went from one plantation to another depending on the need. He would have to do a little politicking with his relatives before he could begin changing the treatment of his slaves.

"Marc, I need someone to run my research and medicinal garden for me. Do we have anyone who could handle that?"

"I can't think of anyone right off hand, but I'll think about it," Marc said.

"Belle was telling about her man, Jules. Do you know him?"

"Yes, he would probably be good at it. He always has a real good garden."

Jean spent the rest of the day riding over the plantation and thinking about crops, slavery and the treatment of slaves. Slaves provided about half of their own food by planting and tending a garden on Sundays. They were encouraged to tend their gardens and not go to church. In some parts of the northern plains Catholicism was taught to the slaves but in most parts of Saint-Domingue slaves were not taught anything about the Christian religion. It was too revolutionary. They might want better treatment or, God forbid, their freedom as a religious right, so old African ways were never extinguished. These ancient ways included voodoo, ancient rites, and a long African history of slavery.

Evening time drifted over the plantations and brought its blend of colors and smells. Sunset hues of purple and pink spread over the savannas and plantations. The evening breeze brought a slight ocean scent that mingled with the floral flagrancies. Jeanne took a deep breath and closed her eyes as she and Jean traveled in their carriage. They were on their way to Jean's Uncle's Ores' house, about two or three miles away. Jean's other uncle, Jean Baptiste Formy, who owned *La Blanchette* Plantation, would also be there. He was a crusty old colonist who had served in the military and developed a sense of management that embraced strict discipline.

"Louis didn't seem to mind that we were leaving him for the evening," Jean said.

"No, he didn't," Jeanne said with a little bit of surprise in her voice. "He really seems to like Belle and Zoé. I thought that after being so close for the last few weeks he might have a harder time with us leaving for a evening."

"No, didn't bother him a bit", Jean said, as they pulled up in front of his uncle's house. "Remember to humor Jean Baptiste. He's quite opinionated."

Jean was helping Jeanne out of the carriage, when the whole Formy clan burst out the front doors to welcome them again. It was as if they had not seen them on the night of their arrival.

Jean Baptiste, Jean's uncle, was definitely the head of the family down here on the island. He was jovial but one could imagine the temper that could be on the other side of those sharp blue-grey eyes. He always wore remnants of his old French military uniform. He had been a general. He had a white beard but kept it closely trimmed. His wife, Marguerite, had died of yellow fever shortly after they arrived on the island seven or eight years ago. The plantations and the family were his sole interest.

The family dined in elegant style with a servant behind every person. It was as an elegant a dinner, even by European standards. Course after course was served and dinner ended with the women staying in the parlor to socialize and the men going out on the veranda to sit, smoke, talk, and enjoy the evening breeze.

The men's conversation covered everything from the political climate in France to local plantation life. They listened in rapped attention as Jean told his story of the firing squad and their subsequent escape to Saint-Domingue. Jean was a good story teller and he made the story last for over an hour. Everyone thoroughly enjoyed it and they toasted drink after drink to their dangerous escape and safe arrival. Jean Baptiste started telling Jean how the plantations were run, how they treated their slaves, and all the unofficial policies of both farm and slave.

"Now, I run my land with a firm hand," Jean Baptiste said. "You can work your slaves twelve to fourteen hours a day, six days a week, feed and clothe with only what you have to and you can get your investment back on the cost of the slave in two or three years. Everything past that is pure profit."

"Jean Baptiste," Jean said. "There is some new thinking back in France that the slaves ought to be treated better. They say..."

"New thinking be damned!" shouted Jean Baptiste. "Those radicals back in France don't know a mango from a goat. They think they have all the answers. They've disposed the King and Queen, turned over all the rules, and they think they are going to tell us what to do down here. Well, I'm going to tell you that there is not one colonist who'll support their ideals down here. And another thing, nobody pays any attention to those damned commissioners they send over, trying to convert us to that new radical thinking." Jacobins," he spat out. "Hang'um all."

No one dared argue with him, much less say anything for a few moments. Jean could tell that even though

124

everyone agreed with his royalist thinking, they did not all agree with his theories of slave treatment. Better treatment meant better return on investment and a longer time before a replacement cost had to be expended. His relatives were here for the long run and the better treatment, if only slightly better, made more sense. Most colonists wanted to stay four or five years, make their fortune, and get back to France. Therefore ninety percent of all plantations had no problem with working their slaves to death.

Jean spoke up after a respectful pause, "Jean Baptiste, I'm willing to wager you that I could work my slaves from sunrise to evening meal five days a week, work them a half day on Saturday, give them more food, not use the whip and I will get just as much out of them as you do."

"Ha, I can hear your father talking," Jean Baptiste said in a huff.

"Yes, that's his thinking. Not only is it his thinking but that is what he wishes me to do here." Jean turned toward his Uncle Ores, "We have more money than we can spend now. Why should we make other people's lives miserable? Just so we can compare our money pile to our neighbor's?"

"You call them people; next you'll tell me they have souls," Uncle Ores said.

"The Church says they do," Jean said.

"Well, no priest down here better say so!" Jean Baptiste snapped back.

A long silence followed with Uncle Ores standing against the veranda railing, looking out on his sugar cane fields. Finally he turned around and shouted "Hell", broke into a smile and said, "Your father and I have had this same argument before and neither one of us changed each other's mind. So what difference does it make? I'm glad you are here. Do what you want with your slaves. I'm sure some of the others here," he stopped and glared at them, "want to do the same."

Jean Baptiste walked over to Jean, gave him a big hug and drinks were toasted again.

The ride home was late but went quickly with Jean trying to explain his brother, Jean Baptiste to Jeanne. They soon arrived at their house and entered after turning over the reins to one of the stablemen. Jeanne went upstairs to check on Louis and found him sleeping. Belle sat in the corner knitting by candlelight.

Belle stood up and met Jeanne at the door and whispered, "He went to sleep soon after dark."

Jeanne went to his bed and kissed him and came back toward Belle. She stopped suddenly and grabbed the door frame to keep her balance.

"Ohhh, I must have exhausted myself," Jeanne said with a small laugh.

"Yes maybe, but you're going to have another baby," Belle said.

Jeanne looked at Belle with amazement. "I haven't even told Jean yet. I wanted to wait another week or two to be sure. How did you know?"

"I just know. No use waiting. You're pregnant," Belle said as she turned to walk down the hall.

Jean had reached the top of the stairs when he saw Belle coming down the hall, smiling.

"Evening, Belle."

"Evening, Dr. Jean."

"Belle, tell Jules not to go in the fields tomorrow. Have him meet me after breakfast out by the barns. Tell him I'm going to try him out as my new assistant in my medicinal garden."

126

"I'll sure tell him, Dr. Jean. He'll be glad to hear it." Belle said. Inside she was filled with excitement, but she tried not to show it.

Jules had to squint as he looked out into the bright morning sun. It was getting hot now. He had been out in the garden since sunrise waiting on the doctor and the early morning coolness was giving way to the heat. He had hardly slept during the night. This was an important assignment and he wanted to make sure that he did everything he could do to appear responsible so the new master would know he was taking his duty seriously. This was important to him. A job like this meant he probably would not die in the next few years.

"Good morning, Jules," Jean said.

Jules was startled and jumped when he heard the voice. He had not seen nor heard anyone walking toward him. Jean had come up behind him from around the barn.

"You gave me a start Monsieur Formy-Duval. I didn't hear you coming. I must have been thinking about the garden," Jules stammered out, trying to recover his composure.

"First, call me Dr. Jean, and second don't be scared of me. We're going to have fun with this garden. It may be work but I think it will be something you'll enjoy."

"That sounds mighty good to me, Dr. Jean," Jules said.

"Let's walk around the garden area and barns and I'll talk about what I want to do with them, then we'll walk down to that piece of swampy ground over there and I'll explain how it's going to tie into our garden."

For the next hour they walked over the grounds and Jean explained how he wanted to use the garden to grow the seed for certain upcoming crops and how he wanted to convert some of the smaller barns into nurseries. He wanted to use the healthiest looking plants in his fields and experiment with plants that showed exceptional growth rates. They walked to the swampy area where Jean started talking about his real passion.

"Do you see that plant with the yellow spotted leaves?" Jean asked. Jules nodded his head. "That is a special plant. It cures headaches."

"No, Dr. Jean, that plant will kill you if you eat it."

"Not if you cook it first, and dilute it with a sugar paste. There are dozens of plants in this one little area that can be used as medicine and I have found many more I want to experiment with. Jules, this is what I really like about being a doctor, the making of medicine. Once we have found plants that work, we are going to grow them as small crops and make medicines out of them. Half of your garden may be crop seedlings but the other half will be a small row of this and a small row of that, whatever we find that works as a medicinal cure."

They finished around mid-morning and Jules had plenty of instructions as to what to do for the next few weeks, modifying barns, using his carpentry skills to build special planting boxes, tools, and the construction of a fence for the garden area. Jules could hardly believe his luck. He could not have picked anything that he would rather do more. His tribe had been the *Aradas* of West Africa. They were well-known for their farming skills, and his family had been good at it. He could hardly wait to tell Belle and Zoé.

Zoé was walking through the Caribbean forest. She occasionally pushed a large leaf or small branch out of the way of her face. She did not want anything to touch her hair. She had it tied up in a bun on her head. Her mother had wanted to know why she had been brushing her hair and preening herself so carefully, but she had no sooner asked the question when Belle knew the answer.

"You going to see Bando this evening?" Belle asked.

"*Oui, Mama.*"

Belle pretended to be busy around the room, trying to understand why Zoé was being more particular about her looks tonight than usual. She was afraid she knew why. Finally she said, "You better stop messing with your hair. It'll be dark soon."

"Mama, I want to look right tonight. This is a special night for me. I may not be back until late." Zoé decided to let her mother know what she intended tonight.

Belle sat down beside Zoé and said, "You going to give yourself to that man tonight?"

Zoé didn't reply but pretended to be concentrating on getting her hair up in a perfect bun.

"Mon cher, you know we've talked about this. You know that once you start you will not be able to stop him or yourself. You'll be tied to him. Life can be so much easier with the right man."

Zoé turned, took her mother's hands in hers and said, "Mama, listen to me. I've seen all them men and I've compared them all to Bando. He is my choice. He is the man I want. All those other rich men just want someone to be a pretty prize holding on to their sleeve. I would be a possession to them, Mama, just like one of their prized horses."

"You don't think Bando would want to show you off?" Belle said.

"I certainly hope so. But he's different. He simply can't live without me. His eyes are powerful and passionate when they're on me. There will be times in our lives when our voices may disagree, but I will never doubt the love in his heart."

Belle sighed with resignation and said, "Oh child."

"Mother, they won't let us marry, they sell our children, and they can take our lives, but they can't take this night from me. I'm going to him and give him a night that will seal our souls together so tight that only God could separate us."

Zoé wiped the tears on her mother's cheek and said, "Be happy for me Mama, be happy, this is what I want."

"I am, I am," Belle said through small sobs. "I'm happy that you've grown so wise."

Zoé kissed her again and went toward the door.

Belle sat there and quietly said, "I love you cher, I love you."

Zoé stopped at the door and looked back at her mother and said, "I love you too, Mama."

Zoé pushed back the last branch that stood between her and the pool at the waterfall. It was a remote place that people knew but seldom took the time to come because of its remoteness. Zoé stopped and looked at it. She never failed to be fascinated by its beauty. The small waterfall that poured into the large pool of water reflected the last rays of the sunset and many of the evening flowers were opening. This was her special place that she shared only with Bando.

She was glad Bando was not here yet. She had the evening written out in her mind and she wanted to prepare the setting before Bando arrived. Whenever he arrived and walked out of the forest on the other side of the pool, she wanted the image of her to be seared in his mind.

She removed her clothes and laid them on a rock near

the falls. She walked out into the pool and submerged herself up to her neck and then waded back to where she was about knee deep. She positioned herself where she would be in front of the white cascading falls when he came out of the woods. Every feature of her would be outlined. She turned profile to what she thought would be his entry point and first sight of her. She took the leg that would be nearest him and placed it on an underwater rock so that her ankle was at the water line. She heard him coming.

Bando walked out of the undergrowth and onto the small sandy beach and stopped. Zoé was naked and the sun's last rays were illuminating the glistening water drops that covered her. She had barely let him touch her before, much less revealed herself to him. He thought about sneaking back into the brush and making a noisy entrance so not to embarrass her when she slowly turned her head toward him and smiled.

He was speechless, his heart pounded. She bent over slightly to brush the water off her uplifted knee. By doing so she framed her breasts against a background of falling water. The frame being, her stomach and arms, when her hands touched her uplifted knee. She looked at him again, smiled, and then reached behind her head with both hands; breasts arched forward, and let her hair out of its bun with a shake of her head.

Bando was still speechless. He had never seen such beauty before and she was just standing there, waiting for him. He removed his clothes and waded into the pool toward her.

Now it was Zoé's turn to be excited by the male coming toward her. She had bathed small boys and helped her mother nurse and care for the sick, both female and male.

Charles Patton

She knew what was there but her mother had watched her closely and she had never seen a naked man before. About half way toward her he stopped and turned away from her so he could get a flower floating in the water. As he walked away from her, her eyes were fixed on the muscles in his buttocks and the back of his thighs. She breathed in quickly; she knew women could be lovely but she had never realized that the male body could be so beautiful.

Bando closed on her with flower in hand. When he was in arms' reach she started to lift her arms to him, but he stopped and circled close behind her. He stopped a few inches before his body touched hers and put the flower in her hair. As he was finishing with the flower he leaned into her and he heard her gasp as their bodies touched. He put his hands on her shoulders and stroked her arms with his hands. She felt her neck and face flush. He pulled her close and caressed her breasts. She started to burn. She turned and they locked in a passionate embrace. His kisses set loose an emotional firestorm. Her head was reeling and she was breathing hard. These unknown emotions were both scaring and thrilling her. She was losing strength in her legs and was starting to slide when he caught her. He picked her up in his arms and carried her to the waters' edge and gently placed her on the soft ground. He resumed his passionate advance and she offered no resistance. Her last rational thought before becoming lost to the maelstrom of sexual passion was to wonder at how powerful the act of sex was and how glad she was to be doing it with someone she loved.

Claude Sartre welcomed the sight of Le Harve harbor. He had been gone from France for six months. It was a bittersweet feeling. He was glad to be home but his failure to catching Dr. Formy-Duval ate at him day and night. He had lost twenty pounds off his already lean frame. The search in Canada had been extremely tough. *God help those poor colonists living there*, he thought. The cold and primitiveness of the French-Canadian outposts toughened up anyone who lived there or they died.

He had searched for weeks at every outpost he could reach, especially in the French areas. No one had heard of a family that fit Dr. Formy-Duval's description. In Ontario, where *Le Bordeaux* had taken port and stayed for a few days, no one recalled a family fitting the family's description. He finally concluded that he might not find them in Canada and he caught one of the last ships back to France before winter ended. "Humph," he snorted as he thought to himself, *Even if they did get by me in Canada it would serve them right. Living there is as bad as being hanged.*

He could see buildings that he recognized now, activity of sailors in the port and could feel the pleasures of being home wash over him. He would sit, drink, and talk to his friends on the Committee and try to figure out where he had missed Dr. Formy-Duval. Then he would trace the doctor down and have him executed. It might take months or years, but news about the doctor and his family would eventually leak out and then he would finally have Dr. Formy-Duval, and all the recognition that he deserved.

Charles Patton

"Nations of Europe, your slaves will break the yoke that weights upon them.
The Negroes only lack a leader.... The old world as well as the new will
applaud him. The name of the hero who will have re-established the rights of
the human species will be blessed forever".
Abbé Raynal, about 1770

A CURE FOR INDEPENDENT THINKING
Summer, 1791

Governor Blanchelande, France's chief government official in Saint-Domingue, had managed to leave Cap Francais before sunrise with only two mounted soldiers as escort for his carriage. He wanted to arouse as little suspicion as possible for this clandestine mission. One plain carriage and two mounted soldiers would scarcely raise an eyebrow on the northern plains.

His mission in Saint-Domingue was a difficult one. He was to keep the island as profitable as possible for France. This meant keeping the slaves at work but the more difficult task was keeping the royalist plantation owners loyal to the new and radical Jacobin Government.

Had the King been in full power, the colonists would feel a little less like revolting, but the new Jacobin government, of which he was an appointee, was much more radical in its thinking toward the colonies and the blacks.

The new French government despised the royalists and almost all plantation owners had royalist sympathies. The Jacobins would be willing to give the slaves more freedoms if they could control the colonists. Recently there was so much talk of revolution and independence in the area that something had to be done before the colonists ran him and his officials off the island.

He and his cabinet had an idea that should dampen the colonists' desire for independence. It was an old trick that the Third Estate had used back in France. Whenever the Third Estate (industrialists, finacialists, and merchants) wanted something from the King, they discreetly incited supposedly spontaneous riots. These had included the storming of the Bastille, the peasant revolts for food, the women's march on Versailles, among others. These outbursts did well if one could keep control over the riotous actors involved in the dissent. If he could stage a small slave rebellion, then the fearful colonists would feel the need for the mother country's protection of militia and government and lose their desire for independence.

He was now pulling into the entrance of Bréda plantation where Bayon de Libertat was the plantation's manager. Bayon was not like the other plantation owners. He, along with the owners of the plantation, was not entirely out for money. He had explicit instructions for lenient treatment of slaves. He believed in this philosophy himself and ran one of few indulgent plantations on the island. Because of his lack of zeal for immediate profits, his political ideals were more moderate; therefore he did not fit in with the rest of the plantation owners and tended to lean toward the present government.

The Governor knew of the Bayon de Libertat's leanings and he knew that one of his slaves was considered influential among the blacks. He wanted to run his plan by Bayon and see if he would help.

Toussaint was walking from the stables toward the house when he saw the carriage turn into the lane leading to the main house. His interest was immediate as soon as he saw the horses pulling the carriage and the mounts ridden by two soldiers. These were not ordinary people because these were not ordinary horses. He could tell even from a distance that these were some of the finest horses on the island. Toussaint rushed to the front of the house to take over the job of handling the horses. This was not so much to see who the people were, but to handle the horses.

He always compared every horse he saw with his own, Belle Argent. It really belonged to Bayon de Libertat, but that was in name only. He fed, groomed, and exercised the horse. The horse looked to him as master. Belle Argent was the best horse he had ever seen in his life and he was proud to be its master.

The man in the carriage and the two soldiers dismounted and were shown into the house. Toussaint and the driver tied the horses and brought water for them. The driver did not mind that Toussaint walked around the horses inspecting them. He wanted to sit down and drink some cool water. Toussaint ran his hands over the necks and haunches of the horses. He talked to them and told them of Belle Argent. He even stuck up a conversation with the driver about the horses. The driver was taken back at first with the slave's easy manner with the French language and his knowledge of horses, but they soon had a light discussion going on about the quality of horses on Saint-Domingue versus those in France.

The driver was about to go into a long glorification of French horseflesh when de Libertat came out on the front porch and called to Toussaint, "Oh, Toussaint, I'm glad you're here. Come inside; we want to talk to you."

Toussaint was at a loss for a few seconds. This was the Governor of St. Domingue and they wanted to talk to *him*.

"It's all right; don't worry. We want you to listen to something," Bayon reassured.

Toussaint entered the parlor with a certain amount of fear. A powerful man wanting to talk to him could only mean trouble. Bayon took him by the arm and gently coerced him toward the governor. "Governor," Bayon said, "I would like to introduce you to Francois Dominique Toussaint."

The governor smiled at Toussaint and politely nodded his head but did not offer his hand. "Toussaint," the governor said. "I have heard much about you and I am glad to finally make your acquaintance." Toussaint could only nod his head. "Please sit down," the governor indicated with his hand, "I would like to discuss a serious matter of business with you."

Toussaint and Bayon seated themselves in chairs opposite from the governor.

The governor looked Toussaint in the eye and after a dramatic pause began speaking. "How would you like to help gain a few extra privileges for your people? Let me tell you what I have in mind. I need a man of your race to lead a small orderly rebellion against the plantation owners."

Toussaint thought, *I'll going to be dead before the sun sets today.*

The governor, seeing the alarm in Toussaint's face, smiled and said, "Don't be alarmed. This will be with the government's secret approval. I need someone who can contact other slaves with leadership ability and coordinate a small but controlled revolt. The slaves will withdraw to the mountains, the government will make a big fuss about it and as an enticement to settle matters, the government will give your people an extra day of rest and prohibit the use of the whip. In addition, you and the leaders of the revolt will be given your freedom. Now, to help organize and finance this little campaign, I have made arrangements for 650,000 francs to be at your disposal."

The governor paused for a moment to let all this sink in and then continued, "Bayon de Libertad seems to think that you are the man who is most capable of carrying this out. Are you that man?"

"No reprisals?" Toussaint asked cautiously.

"Absolutely none."

"What makes you think I can keep the rebellion under control?"

"Makes no difference. If you can't, then the government can."

"Can I think about this for a while?"

"Think quickly. Bayon will show me around his plantation. When we come back we can talk some more and you can tell me your decision." The governor stood up and indicated that he was ready for his tour and they all walked outside. Toussaint walked outside near the garden and sat down under a large shade tree to think.

For the next hour Toussaint thought of possibilities, evaluated ideas and weighed ramifications. He desperately wanted to gain the extra day and the elimination of the whip for his people. But he did not really believe that if it failed, or the revolt spun out of control, that he would be held blameless.

He was still sitting under the tree when the governor and Bayon approached him. "Well, Toussaint, what is your decision?" the governor asked.

Toussaint stood up and faced the men. "Governor, if I can make this revolt happen and stay in the background and not be in the leadership, would that be acceptable?"

The governor smiled. He knew this was the man. Here was a man who wanted to organize the rebellion but desired to stay out of the limelight so as not to be held responsible. A real politician. "Yes," the governor said, "that would be acceptable. Now let's talk about some details."

The next two hours were spent deciding what each side expected of each other and how the campaign would be financed. When the discussion was over, Bayon went back into the house and Toussaint leaned against a fence and watched the governor and his two officers ride off.

He already had in his mind the men that he thought could lead the revolt. He would start riding tomorrow. He would have to contact each man after dark. It would take a good month to contact each man and another month or two to orchestrate the details. He needed to talk to Suzanne.

Charles Patton

Les Bois Caïman
(*The Caïman Woods*)

The darkness of the glen worried Toussaint. Everywhere he looked he could only see a partial face here and a pair of eyes there. Torches glowed near the center of the gathering. Over two hundred representatives were seated in a semicircle. He knew two black men from every northern plain plantation were here. It was Sunday and each man had walked most of the day to get to this late night assemblage.

Toussaint saw his nephew approaching and called his name, "Moyse."

Moyse, who was blind in one eye, had trouble finding Toussaint. "Toussaint," he said, relieved to finally spot him."

"Are all the people I assigned to you coming?" Toussaint asked. Moyse was Toussaint's favorite nephew in whom he had absolute trust. Many contact assignments had been assigned to him.

"Yes, I think so. Everyone I contacted promised they would be here."

"Do they know the way?"

"Yes. If they had any doubts, I gave them a name of a contact nearby to them. Someone they could join up with who knew the way."

"Good, good" Toussaint said, relieved. A good turnout showed that every contact felt as strongly about the cause as he did.

Moyse looked around and said, "Are all the leaders

140

here? Boukman and all the others?"

"I arrived a few moments before you, but yes, I think they're all here."

"Was it hard to get them to come?"

"No, that part was easy. They're all for change and a revolt."

"What do you mean, *that part*?"

"Well, the hard part was not convincing them to come or even to be one of the leaders. What they had trouble with was the fact that I was only organizing the meeting and not taking part in the leadership."

"What wrong with that?"

"They're suspicious that I'm setting them up in a trap."

"Oh, I see."

"I convinced most of them that a fifty year-old man is too old to be leading this revolt and that I really don't want any responsibility or least not right now."

"Did they believe you?"

"I think most of them do, except for Boukman. He's suspicious of anything that breathes and will kill anyone at the smallest provocation."

The truth was that Toussaint was a careful man and he wanted to separate himself from the situation until he saw that it was going to be successful and for the most part a peaceful revolution.

Thunder muttered in the background and the heavy clouds made the sultry night darker than normal. Boukman, a tall man with a compelling presence, stepped forward and the gathering trembled with anticipation. Boukman was the man whom Toussaint knew would rise to the top and become the natural leader. He was Jamaican, a voodoo priest, and ruthless. In a moment he would speak and at that moment Boukman would become the leader of the revolution and any part that he, Toussaint, might have had in organizing the revolution would not matter. He stepped a little further back into the woods. It was time for him to go. According to his plan he should not even be here. It was hard to see his plan leave his hands completely, but it was his choice not to be so closely involved; he turned and started walking back to Bréda.

"BROTHERS," Boukman cried out in Creole. "I am your friend."

"Brother," the crowd shouted back.

"My brothers," Boukman said. "Our King and friend in France has issued a command that gives us another day of freedom during the week so that we can work our gardens to feed ourselves." His voice slowly rose, "But would the white planters agree to this? No! They are ignoring their own King, who is God's messenger on earth. They have ignored all edicts that protect us but now it is different. The King is sending an army to enforce his wishes and punish the planters. It is now time for us to strike the first blow. We should strike and then wait in the mountains for the King's men to come."

Boukman turned to a mulatto assistant and had him read a newspaper concerning the King's edict. The article, written precisely for this meeting and having almost no truth in it, was read to the assembly. It told of how displeased the King was with the colonists and that he was sending an army to correct the situation. The crowd listened intently, and was becoming excited by the reading.

Boukman was pleased with the crowd's reaction. After the clerk finished the reading Boukman stood silently, arms folded, in front of the audience for a few moments. "Brothers, what needs to be done? Give me your thoughts."

One of the older, wiser men spoke up, "Maybe we should wait for the French Army to arrive and see if they will take care of the problem. It might save some of our lives."

This was not what Boukman wanted to hear. He knew that the French Army was not coming so he recognized others in the crowd whom he knew were ready for quick action. After ten minutes the crowd had reached Boukman's point of view. They were ready for military action, *now*.

"Brothers, wait. There is still much to be done and prepare for. We will strike on the next full moon. Messengers will soon contact you and tell you what you need to know.

The decision to take the first step was now agreed upon. Boukman led the assembly, not only down a path into a tight compact jungle cove where the voodoo priestess Damballa and her altar lay, but also into a pact that many in the crowd thought was with the devil, a pact that has wreaked havoc on Saint-Domingue for two hundred years.

Damballa was tall and gaunt with wild steaks of grey through her hair. Everyone gathered around the altar for this ritual where a pig was bound. Damballa, with a long knife in hand, raised both hands to the rumbling sky. She paused and waited; everyone held their breath. Then when Damballa thought the moment was right, she started her downward movement of the knife into the pig. At the precise moment she plunged the knife, lightning struck nearby and the resulting thunder not only shook everyone but convinced them that some deity, God or Devil, was surely looking on their actions.

The priestess cut the pig's throat and two assistants caught the blood in cups. They mixed it with rum and gunpowder and passed it around as if it were a communal cup.

It was now time for people to leave and Boukman dramatically raised his arms to the sky which was producing lightning and thundering continuously and shouted out a powerful parting benediction, *"The God who created the sun which gives us light, the God who rouses the waves and rules the storms, though he is hidden in the clouds, he watches over us. He beholds the deeds of the whites. The white man's God inspires him with crimes; our God calls upon us to do good works. Our God is merciful but he wishes us to be avenged. He will direct our arms and aid us. Throw away the symbol of the God of the whites, that God who gloats over our suffering, and NOW listen to the voice of liberty, which finds an echo in our hearts."*

Suddenly his arms fell to his side as if God had been holding on to them while he was talking and then suddenly released them. The assembly murmured their amens and melted back into the woods to return to their plantations.

La Plaine du Nord Explodes

Toussaint had ridden Belle Argent most of the afternoon in order to be near the Flaville Plantation, the first designated point of attack. He had stayed on the main roads until he came near the general area of the plantation. He then took wooded trails so as not to be seen approaching the plantation. It was early evening and he needed to make contact with the black leaders hiding just south of the plantation.

He had Belle Argent at a slow walk along a narrow path when a sentry stepped out and motioned for him to dismount and follow him. Within a few minutes the sentry had led him into a small clearing where the leaders from the other plantations were gathered. Chief among them was Boukman, who gave him an arrogant look of condescension and motioned to a place for him to wait. Even though Toussaint had actually orchestrated the rebellion so far, Boukman was not about to let him have any further power or appear influential. This was just as well with Toussaint, since he did not want his name to be associated with the start of the rebellion or any repercussions from it. He had struggled with the decisions to be there at all, but he finally decided to help make sure that tonight's actions would not get out of hand.

Boukman and other leaders made their way onto the Flaville Plantation around ten o'clock and gave his first order. "Send runners to the slave quarters and let them know we are here."

Slaves from the plantation and surrounding plantations ran out from their huts with machetes in hand and marched toward the main house.

The manager of the plantation ran out with whip in hand. When he perceived the magnitude of the problem he beat a hasty retreat to the main house, barricading all inside and made ready for a siege with all available weapons.

Slaves were lighting torches and making menacing glances toward the house when Toussaint decided to see if he could avoid the violence by making an appeal, "Boukman, we have the slaves; they're free now. Let's see if we can avoid destroying as much property as possible. We might need the plantations later."

Boukman shrugged his shoulders in indifference, gave the men with torches a disapproving look, and signaled to the group that they were to move to the next plantation. All the slaves from the Flaville plantation joined and Boukman's army started to grow.

At the next two plantations it was the same as the Flaville plantation. The slaves joined the revolt with no harm or damages to the plantations, nor to the white owners and managers.

At the next plantation a white manager ventured too close to the crowd and was captured. Boukman was ready for the crowd to have their way with him.

Again Toussaint stepped in. "Boukman, we haven't killed anyone yet. Let's not incite the colonists beyond reason."

Boukman gave Toussaint a look of distain but then signaled for the men to let the manager go, but he was getting tired of Toussaint's suggestions. It interfered with his appearance of leadership.

At this point, as if to show Toussaint who was boss, Boukman called for an election to select a leader. Boukman felt, that with all the new slaves that had joined his army, they needed to know who the leader was. In a hasty vote Boukman was elected leader by acclamation.

Toussaint remained on the fringes and interjected his gentle guidance on the group only when leniency was needed. He dared not interfere with Boukman's rule, less he became a target of the merciless Boukman himself.

The Noé Plantation was next. Runners were again sent into the slave quarters and the slaves soon accepted their freedom and joined the revolt.

The slaves on this plantation had been treated particularly bad and lived in horrible conditions, even by Saint-Domingue standards. When they gathered around Boukman's guards, the slaves grabbed some of the torches and started for the main plantation house.

Toussaint turned and took a step toward Boukman. Boukman snapped his head toward Toussaint with a look that said, "Don't interfere!"

The mob, with torches and machetes in hand, charged the house. They were intent on taking their revenge. The owner and overseer were killed, but a doctor and his wife who lived in the main house were spared. The house was ransacked, someone torched a curtain and the house went up in flames.

When the rest of the slaves saw the plantation house burning, a great feeling of justice and satisfaction was released within them and to feed this feeling soon all the buildings on the plantation were torched along with the sugar cane fields.

Here the leaders of the revolt lost complete control.

Within a couple of days most the plantations on the northern plain of Saint-Domingue were burned, temporarily blocking out the sun and moon. Ships coming into Cap Francais could see the smoke miles before they arrived at the harbor. Over a 100,000 slaves had claimed their freedom and joined the revolt.

Within two months, 220 sugar plantations, 600 coffee plantations, and almost 200 cotton and indigo plantations were destroyed. Two thousand whites and 10,000 blacks were killed. Extreme atrocities were committed by both sides. The whites flocked to the cities for safety. The blacks that had chosen not to participate in the revolt were forced to live in the rebel camps just to be safe. About 10,000 whites and mulattoes gathered within and around Cap Francais for safety but were stunned to see that they were surrounded by 40,000 slaves, which was less than half of the total slave army.

The Crousilleau Plantation as well as all the other plantations in the southern part of Saint-Domingue had received the news with much fear. Each night the Formy and Crousilleau families would meet on their verandas and discuss the latest news from the northern plains.

"Jean, do you think the revolt will come here and what will we do if it does?" asked Jeanne.

"I don't think it will reach this far. No slave down here has that kind of following; besides, since the trouble up north started the owners down here have been extra diligent in watching out and taking care of any troublemakers."

"But what if it does come, what will we do?"

"We may have to flee Saint-Domingue."

"Where to?"

Jean thought for a minute and said, "We cannot go back to France. We would be considered Royalists, friends of the

King, and they are beheading them everywhere. We would have to flee somewhere else in the Caribbean or perhaps New Orleans."

This did not satisfy Jeanne's fears. Down deep, like any other person, what she wanted most was a safe place for her children to live.

Charles Patton

Madame de Libertat

During the first two or three months of the rebellion Toussaint's desire was to stay in the background and not be perceived as a leader of the slave revolt. He had done what Governor Blanchelande had asked, started a minor revolt to scare the white plantation owners and make them show more loyalty and feel the need of the government's protection, but the Governor and his cabinet were not unlike a person who wanting to start a fire to burn out the underbrush had started a forest fire. It had shaken both the government and Toussaint.

Toussaint returned to Bréda Plantation to wait with his family. While there he began to fear for the safety of the plantation owner's wife. Bayon de Libertat had gone to Cap Francais on business a couple of weeks before the revolt started and had asked Toussaint to look after his wife's safety. Toussaint knew that while the slaves at their plantation would not harm Madam de Libertat, his influence could not hold off a black invasion much longer.

One morning he approached the madam in her garden and said, "Excuse me, Madam, but your husband asked me to look after you while he is gone and I can no longer guarantee your safety."

"What do you mean? Are you saying that I should leave?"

"*Oui*, Madam, I cannot protect you much longer. You must leave for your own safety. I will have my brother, Paul, pack your things and he and several men from the plantation will accompany you to Cap Francais."

"Do you really think it has come to this, that I must leave my own home?"

"*Oui* Madam, it has come that far. You must leave. It has become dangerous for you here."

A tear rolled down her cheek. "Very well, when should I leave?"

"Tomorrow morning, Paul will have you packed. He and some men of your loyal slaves will accompany you to the entrance of Cap Francais."

Madam de Libertat left the next morning escorted by her slaves, who were also her friends, and made it safely to Cap Francais where she joined her husband. In the meantime, Toussaint took his own family to safety across the border in the Spanish Territory of San Domingo.

Toussaint decided that now was the time to join the rebellion. After a month in San Domingo he came back across the border and into Saint-Domingue. He located the rebel encampment and found that it was run by three generals. Boukman was not one of them. He had been captured and hanged. Toussaint also found four priests and several white, former generals, acting as advisors. The black generals, wary of Toussaint because of his leadership potential, assigned him the duty and title of, *Doctor to the King's Armies*. Toussaint performed his duties so well that even the jealous generals assigned him more and more important tasks with actual military responsibility. Soon he was a general and in command of part of the army.

Toussaint had received intelligence that three new commissioners were arriving from France to help govern the country. It was also rumored that a French Army was to follow soon after their arrival.

Toussaint had gently urged and finally convinced the

generals of the Black Army to try negotiating with the government to establish a peace agreement.

Envoys were sent back and forth between the local government and the black leaders. Toussaint and the generals asked that four hundred of the black leaders be given their freedom, that the slaves be given an extra free day during the week, and that the whip be prohibited.

When the colonists balked at the idea of liberty for the four hundred black leaders, Toussaint offered the idea of only sixty leaders being set free.

The Colonial Assembly scoffed at the peace offerings, treated the emissaries rudely, and dismissed them.

When the two emissaries returned to camp and reported the results, the black generals became enraged and ordered all the white captives killed. Toussaint was able to talk the generals out of this order.

Toussaint spoke with Father Delahaye, one of the priests who was acting as an advisor, "How can the government not meet our requests? They are so small in comparison to what they get in return, peace and a return to normal life."

Father Delahaye replied, "Some men cannot deal with change. They want things to be the way they have always been. Men who cannot adapt are the ones who lose the most and the ones who adapt the quickest either become rich or great leaders."

"This has changed my mind about one thing," Toussaint said.

"What is that? asked the Father.

"We cannot have some people in slavery and others free. All have to be free. Whatever it takes, no more slavery in Saint-Domingue!" Toussaint said.

Toussaint and the other black generals worked tirelessly to defeat the French Colonists who were huddled around and in Cap Francais. Within a few weeks they were at the gates of Cap Francais and a quasi-peace was brokered. When the leading elements of the Black Army entered Cap Francais, fires began to break out all over the city. Some said they were started by the blacks and others said by the retreating sailors of the French fleet. It was probably both. Within a couple of days the whites had retreated to the docks. Finally, one night a hundred ships loaded with ten thousand white colonists fled Cap Francais for America.

This large influx of French refugees heavily influenced the passage of the *Alien Enemies Act* in the United States, part of the *Alien and Sedition Acts*, which was passed five years later in 1798. This allowed the President of the United States to deport aliens whose home country is at war with the United States.

Most of these fleeing white colonists settled along the United States' seaboard, especially in the mid-Atlantic and Southern states. Their horrific stories of slave rebellion and atrocities would be etched into the Southern mind and would have a great effect on Southerners' mindset for the next fifty years leading up the American Civil War.

Charles Patton

The Spanish Venture

Toussaint had the foresight to understand that even if the slave revolt was completely victorious, they would have to align themselves with some world power. He wanted it to be France. He was French in thought and mannerisms but he had reservations about the Republicans who now ruled France. They were atheists and had killed the King, who had been a friend to the black man.

Toussaint was a strong Catholic and his many cleric friends had helped him come to his conclusion. Their discussions had also led him to the conclusion that the Spanish, who held the other half of the island, would, in time, take over the island. Therefore, he had decided that he would leave the Black Army and join the Spanish, across the border and help them free all the slaves in Saint-Domingue.

Toussaint was given a commission as a general and an army of 600 men. He began a campaign against the ruling French Colonial Government and won victory after victory. This sounds impressive but at each town or battle, the opposition was normally led by a Colonial officer with a few hundred mulattoes and slaves who would give no opposition to Toussaint and eagerly joined him. He soon had an army of 6,000 men.

Zoé was working her way through the island foliage toward Bando and their secluded meeting place at the falls. She pulled back the last palm frond that hid her from the falls and saw Bando sitting on a boulder near the falls. Usually he was alert and would see her as soon as she emerged from the foliage, but this time he was deep in thought and was not even conscious of her entry into the pool. Zoé took a couple of steps into the pool and then dove into the deeper water.

The sound of the water brought Bando out of his trance and his head snapped around with a smile. "Zoé."

"And what other girl do you think it would be?" Zoé teased.

"You know the one; the prettiest girl on the island."

"Oh, really, and where is this girl?"

"I'm looking at her."

Zoé came out of the water. She gave Bando a kiss, sat down beside him and said, "What were you thinking about so hard? You didn't even hear me come through the forest."

Bando looked down at Zoé's reflection in the water. *This is going to be hard to say*, he thought.

He put his hand behind Zoé's neck, pulled her to him, and gently kissed her. "Zoé, I have been thinking about this for a long time.

"What?" she asked, but her instincts told her that this was not something that she wanted to hear.

Bando dreaded telling her this. He finally looked up and said, "That slave revolt up north, has been going on for several years now and I've stayed here, doing nothing. I'm going up there and join the fight."

"No! Too many people, especially blacks, are getting killed up there. Stay here; there's hardly any fighting down here. Don't go."

"Listen to me Zoé. I've thought about this for a long time. I am going to find General Toussaint's army and join him."

"Why him, for God's sake?"

"I've talked to many people who have been there and know about these things. All the generals are fighting to be free, but Toussaint seems to be fighting for something more than his personal freedom. Some people think he has a better plan for the people.

"I had never thought about it much before, but one of Toussaint's men was here recently, recruiting, and he explained that Toussaint wanted all the people on the island to work together. Toussaint says we have to have the white people's help from outside of our country for the country to be prosperous. The other generals may want freedom, but they are in it for themselves. Some of the generals would like to kill all the mulattoes, that's you Zoé; some want to kill all the whites; and a couple want to kill all the blacks and leave the island for the mulattoes. Toussaint is the only one thinking about the future of the country for everyone."

Zoé sighed, "Sounds like you've thought this about this for a long time. When are you leaving?"

"Tomorrow."

"Tomorrow! So soon", Zoé said. Tears began to flow down her cheeks.

"I would have been gone a long time ago except for you." Bando took both of Zoé's hands and cupped his hands around them and squeezed them gently. "Zoé, listen, what kind of future do we have here? Nothing! We can't even get married. I love you and want to be with you the rest of my life but there has got to be something better."

"But if you go I might not ever see you again," Zoé said.

"Possibly; war is dangerous, but I promise, I will take care of myself and visit every chance I get."

Zoé cried for a few minutes but then they kissed and Zoé made love to him; not him to her. She made the lovemaking as passionate as she could. She wanted him to come back to *her*, not some slave girl he might find up north.

Bando's trip to the northern plains took about two months. He traveled at night; begged food from slaves, who barely had enough for themselves and slept in beds of leaves and sugar cane husks. He tried to keep his mind blank and if he had to think, he tried to think of nothing but of Toussaint and his army.

After walking most of the night he would lay down to sleep before dawn, and then the image of Zoé would creep into his mind as he drifted into a light sleep. She would come to him and rest his head in her lap. He could see her camel-colored skin and her almond shaped, greenish-brown eyes. His tired body would relax and go into a sound sleep as her hands caressed his hair and temples.

During the journey he had to be careful about which black encampments he entered. If he walked into the wrong one, then he would be drafted into that general's army and not be allowed to leave.

Toussaint was a popular general and Bando had no trouble getting information as to where he was encamped, but even with good information Toussaint was hard to find because he moved so fast and often.

One morning Bando was awakened by the sound of men and horses marching down a road. He crept close to the road and soon gathered enough courage to ask one of the men who they were.

With pride the man told Bando that he was one of Toussaint's soldiers and this was his army. Bando stepped in stride with the men and that evening he was assigned to General Moyse's command, one of Toussaint's aides and nephew.

It took a few weeks, but Bando was soon assigned to Moyse's personal staff. He was not an officer; he had become Moyse's chief sergeant. It was his job to take the general staff's commands and relay it to the common soldier. He had to make them understand what needed to be done and make it happen.

Bando had been with Toussaint's army for several months and had fought in several battles against the French and French Colonists. He had learned how to load and shoot both pistols and long-barreled muskets, but his personal favorite was the sword. He was taking lessons, from an ex-French army officer. Soon he was an accomplished swordsman. It seemed natural in his hand, maybe from years of wielding a machete in the sugar cane fields.

One of Bando's duties was to teach recruits how to load and fire a musket. He was working with some recruits one afternoon when he saw Moyse approaching him. "Bando, come to headquarters tonight; we need to discuss an upcoming battle with the English."

This struck Bando as strange because they had only fought the French up until now. "Why are we fighting the English?"

"Because they have captured most of our coastal ports. This blocks the ships that supply us with arms from America. Also, French and American ships can't get through to buy sugar and coffee from Saint-Domingue. We have to have foreign currency flowing into the country."

"But why would the English invade us?"

"The French and English are always at fighting each other. They'll do anything to hurt the French commerce."

That evening, after the battle plans had been discussed and most of the staff had left, Bando noticed Toussaint seemed perplexed and deep in thought.

He had developed a speaking relationship with Toussaint and decided to see if he needed anything. "General, is there anything I can get for you?"

"No, Toussaint said, "I'm trying to make up my mind about a problem."

"Problems with the Colonists?" Bando asked.

"It's not only them; it's the whole situation. The black generals want freedom just for themselves. They want to have things the way they were, except, *they* would be the plantation owners with slaves. The Spanish Government, who I now work for, has changed its mind and is advocating freedom for only for a few blacks, keeping slavery as it was. Then there is the English. France, Spain, and England are all at war with one another and England has taken the opportunity to invade Saint-Domingue. They have successfully done so in almost all coastal towns, especially ones with large harbors. The English have no desire for total freedom for the slaves. They want to contain the revolt so it doesn't spread to Jamaica."

"So what are you going to do?" Bando asked.

"I am thinking about rejoining the French and fighting the black generals, the Spanish, and the English,"

"Do you think they'll take you back, and why the French?" Bando asked.

"Oh yes, they would love to have my army. They send offers to me all the time and even though their local commissioners are not really for freedom, the home government in France does profess freedom for all blacks," Toussaint said.

"You mean we are going to fight the local Colonists, the black generals, and the English?"

"Yes, that is exactly what I am going to do. I will fight

in the interior against whatever army opposes us and with patience I will let malaria and yellow fever take care of the European armies. When they are at their weakest then I'll attack."

"Do you have plans for the southern part of the island?" asked Bando, thinking about Zoé and Crousilleau.

"Yes, after I finish with the English, I will send one of my generals to the south and take control."

"I would like to go with that army when the time comes. I'm from there and I think I can be of assistance."

Toussaint stood and placed his hand on Bando's shoulder, "Good, I'll remember that."

The First Black Government in the

Western Hemisphere

1798

The war was going well for Toussaint. The Spanish had given up and quit several years ago, the black generals had either been killed or fled the country, and that only left the English to deal with, although the southern part of the island was not yet under his control.

Bando rode alongside General Moyse. Toussaint's entire army was marching toward Cap Francais, which had changed hands many times, and Bando could hardly conceal his excitement.

"General, do you think that the colonists will let Toussaint enter Cap Francais?"

Moyse leaned forward and made a small adjustment in his horse's bridle and said, "It's all been arranged. Commissioner Laveaux has made an arrangement with Toussaint. Laveaux had little choice. He knows that Toussaint has enough power to reduce Cap Francais to rubble. Besides, Toussaint would rather conquer by negotiations than battle."

"Well, we'll see, there're the gates to Cap Francais," Bando said.

In a few minutes the army was marching down the main

161

street of Cap Francais. Bando had never seen so many people; they were black, mulatto and white. Everyone was cheering Toussaint. Soon Toussaint found an elevated platform and started giving a speech.

"My compatriots, five years ago I entered this city as a mere slave, driving my master's carriage. Now look at us. I am a general and we are starting a new nation, the first free, black nation in the Western Hemisphere. We will set up government here in this city and we will be equal trading partners with every nation in the world. We will have judges, representatives to an assembly, and everyone can take part in free commerce. We will rule Saint-Domingue as a free nation."

Bando leaned toward Moyse and shouted over the crowd, "This is the proudest day of my life. I can't believe it's happening."

Two weeks later Toussaint took his final step to consolidate power. The last person in his way for total control was French Commissioner Laveaux. He had to take care of Laveaux before he turned his attention toward the English and the southern part of the island. Laveaux and the other French commissioner, Sonthonax, had to leave the island. This was done in short order when Toussaint's troops showed up at the Commissioner's houses' one morning and escorted them to a ship in the harbor that took them to France.

As a result of the commissioner's expulsion the government in France began to fear Toussaint as a rising power, that they would have to deal with someday, even though Toussaint professed his allegiance to France. Toussaint knew of their fears but did not care. Every governor or commissioner that France had sent to the island, since Napoleon recently took power, wanted freedom for the mulattoes only, and to keep the rest of the blacks in slavery. Nobody wanted complete freedom for everyone like Toussaint. He regarded everyone, white, mulatto and black as indispensable to the future of the country. Even his generals had a difficult time with this concept.

Jules was struggling to make everything fit into the wagon he and Dr. Jean were taking to Port-Au-Prince.

"Have you got everything, Jules?" Jean said

"Yes sir, I got the medicines you made up, I got the herbs you want to sell and I got the mortar and pestle," Jules said as he wiped his brow.

"Good, I hope so. We've been experimenting and making medicine for years now and I believe we've have something that we can sell in Port-Au-Prince."

"Yes sir, but it's been selling good around here for years. I don't see why you have to go to Port-Au-Prince to sell it."

"More money, Jules. Those merchants and sailors around the port have money to throw away."

"Dr. Jean, you got plenty of money, why you going to all this extra trouble?"

"I enjoy the excitement of making it work. Starting a new business; growing it on the plantation, experimenting until you get a medicinal potion that works, and then sell it to people who need it."

"Well, some of it works all right, especially that mouth wash. It cures mouth sores real good," Jules said nodding his head in agreement.

Zoé ran out to the wagon and saw that they would soon be on their way to Port-Au-Prince. "Take me, Dr. Jean, please take me too. I can help you sell the medicines in Port-Au-Prince."

"I don't know Zoé; we're going to sell on the streets. We'll be gone at least three or four days and I don't know if Belle would want to let you be gone that long. She depends on you to help run that house and help with the children."

"She'll let me go; I'll go ask," Zoé shouted back over her shoulder as she ran inside the house to find Belle.

Jean raised his hand in protest but she was already in the house. He looked at Jules, and they shrugged and continued packing the wagon.

Belle was not excited with the idea of Zoé going to Port-Au-Prince. Too many men in Port-Au-Prince were sure to notice Zoé's uncommon beauty. Belle had been there before, and she knew that many a brothel owner would scheme to tempt her into staying. Even some married men would offer to put her in a house as a mistress.

Belle turned to Jeanne and said, "Madam Jeanne, don't you think Zoé should stay and help you take care of the children?" Jeanne now had three more children in addition to Louis. There was Jean, Jr., Henrietta, and the baby Alexander, all two years a part.

Jeanne thought for a moment. She did not want to see Zoé go to Port-Au-Price either. It was a wicked city, but Zoé needed to see something of world outside Crousilleau. "Let her go, Belle, we can get one of the other girls to help for a few days."

Belle was reluctant, but gave in. She could not keep Zoé hidden forever, besides Jules and Dr. Jean would be there to protect her. Still, she worried about her. In many ways Zoé was naïve. She did not realize how beautiful she was or could be with only a little work with her hair and clothes.

Belle was sure someone would take notice, but she was a young woman now, and she had to let her live her life.

"All right, Zoé, but see that you stay close to Jules and Dr. Jean and don't be dressing fancy while you are there. There're men there that would think nothing about kidnapping you and selling you off this island."

"Don't worry, Momma, I'll be real careful."

Zoé ran to her cabin and grabbed the only other two pieces of clothing that she owned; a blouse and a skirt, and then ran to the wagon and jumped on top of the baggage.

Jules turned and looked back at Zoé, wondering if she had permission from Belle or not.

"Let's go, Momma said I could."

Jean stepped onto the porch when Jeanne, carrying Louis, and Belle walked out on the porch. He gave Jeanne a kiss and tried to kiss Louis but he hid his head in his mother's shoulder and whimpered.

Jean looked puzzled. "What's the matter with him?

"I don't know, he's been cranky all morning and I think he's starting to run a fever. Jean kissed Jeanne again, felt of Louis head to check for fever. *Maybe*, he thought. He patted Louis on the back on his head and then climbed up in the wagon with Jules.

Jules was ready to go, he popped the reins, and shouted to Belle, "Don't worry, I'll watch Zoé real close. We'll have a good time."

Belle forced a smile and waved back to a beaming Zoé.

It had been almost ten years since Sartre had lost track of Dr. Jean Formy-Duval. The bitterness of the experience had barely diminished and he thought about him almost every day. It finally occurred to him that he should compose a letter and send it to the port master in every

French colony. *Why didn't I think of this before?* he thought. In the letter he described Dr. Formy-Duval, his wife, the fact that they had at least one child, and the date they may have arrived at their destination port. He ended it with a plea to help him find this person and let French justice be satisfied.

Port-Au-Prince

The journey to Port-Au-Prince took most of the day and Zoé, perched on a comfortable piece of baggage, talked the entire time. Jules finally turned to her and said, "Child, could you give our ears a rest for a while?"

"Sorry Daddy, I just can't help it. I bet I'll be too excited to sleep tonight, 'cause tomorrow I get to see Port-Au-Prince."

Jean interjected, "We may not get to see much more of Port-Au-Prince than Market Street. That's where we'll be selling our medicines."

"Why don't you set up a shop and I can operate it for you?"

"Oh yeah, Belle would like that,' Jean said. "Zoé, it'll be easier on all of us if we can convince the merchants to buy from us for resale. Then I don't have the expense of a shop or someone to operate it. If the medicines become popular then demand will run our legs off trying to make it and transport it to Port-Au-Prince.

"I hope people like it and then we can come to Port-Au-Prince every week."

Jules turned his head toward Zoé and put a finger up to his lips.

"OK, Daddy, I'll try to be quiet."

The quietness lasted for another hour, but when they reached the outskirts of Port-Au-Prince she started a monologue that did not stop until they found a place to stay.

Jean found a tavern where he could spend the night but the best he could do for Jules and Zoé was a livery where he stabled the horses. It had a loft with fresh hay where they could sleep. At least, this way Jules could keep an eye on the merchandise.

Jean looked around and scratched his head, "Zoé, I feel bad that I can't do any better for you. What if I go out and get us some bread and cheese?"

"Oh, that sounds good Dr. Jean. I bet they have some fancy breads here."

"I'll go see what I can find."

Jean did manage to find a shop that was about to close their doors. He bought some imported French cheese and some French bread, baked like they do in Paris. Across the street he was able to buy a jug of French wine. It was all a little more than he had planned on, but it eased his conscious about putting Zoé and Jules in a stable.

They spread a cloth over the hay in the upstairs loft and spread the food and wine. Jean cut the bread and cheese while Jules climbed back down to the wagon to get their water cups for the wine.

"Umm," Zoé said, "I've never tasted cheese like this, it wonderful; and that bread is delicious!" she said, as she downed a whole cup of wine.

"Whoaaa girl! That's not water you're drinking. You better sip it along with your bread and cheese," Jean warned. Jules was laughing so hard he could barely speak.

"I've never had wine that tasted so good. Everything about this trip is wonderful; the city, the food, and especially the wine," Zoé said, while pouring herself another cup of wine.

Jean and Jules raised their eyebrows at each other over Zoé's antics and then started a discussion recounting how they had experimented with different herbs; how Jean compounded the ingredients, and how both of them decided on which products to concentrate.

After much reminiscing, Jean raised his cup and toasted Jules, "Here's to the man who works magic in our medicinal garden; a man who has the gift of nature; taught to him by his African ancestors."

Jules raised his glass and said, "And here's to the man who knows how to use them, taught to him by his father." Jules wished Belle could be here to enjoy this with them.

They poured themselves another cup of wine and then both of them stopped and looked at each other. There had not been any background chatter from Zoé in the last few minutes.

They turned their heads toward Zoé. She was passed out in the straw, in a spread eagle position. One hand was holding a piece of cheese and the other an empty wine cup. Jean and Jules exploded into a fit of laughter. Jules thought, *Maybe it's a good thing Belle isn't here.*

The next morning Jules and Zoé finished off the bread and cheese for breakfast, and washed it down with water. When Jean arrived from the tavern he found the horses hitched to the wagon with Jules and Zoé ready to go; although Zoé seemed to be in a slight fog.

About nine o'clock the shops and the open air markets came to life and so did Zoé.

Zoé watched Jean try to make a sale or two, both without success. "Dr. Jean, let me try to sell the next one. I bet I can do it."

Jean had not planned to expose Zoé to the market vendors but if she could sell, then he would see what she could do. "All right, Zoé, you've heard me give the sales talk, so give it a try. Make eye contact and smile." Jean straightened Zoé's hat and plucked some straw out of her hair, "Go," Jean said pointing to the next vendor.

Zoé was a natural, especially if the vendor was a man. She would approach with her head down where the vendor could not see her face, pretending to be giving his merchandise some serious consideration. The vendor would ask if he could help. Then Zoé would spring it on him. She would suddenly bring her face where her hat would no longer be hiding her face. She would look directly into his eyes and start a conversation, which eventually lead to her talking about her sore mouth, which was getting much better due to the medicinal mouthwash she was using.

The vendor was normally so stunned by her eyes and facial beauty that they did not realize that they were being trapped. She never missed a sale, not one.

Jean was fascinated by the way Zoé would spring her beauty on the unsuspecting vendors. *Maybe she's not as naïve as we think she is*, Jean thought.

About mid-afternoon Jean called Zoé over and said, "We've have about half of the merchandise left and we've only covered about a third of the market place. You must be getting tired, let's finish tomorrow."

"One more shop. I want to try that building over there," Zoé said, pointing to a prominent looking apothecary shop.

"Ok, one more shop, and then we go rest and get a good meal."

Zoé entered the shop using her usual head down technique. Two gentlemen were talking, one white merchant, behind the counter and a well-dressed mulatto customer. After a couple of minutes the customer indicated to the merchant to take care of the young lady.

"Good afternoon, can I help you with something?"

Zoé raised her head and started into her sales talk. The

merchant was enchanted but the mulatto customer was mesmerized.

The merchant agreed to buy some of the products and was getting money to pay her when the customer started asking Zoé questions.

"Mademoiselle, who do you work for?"

"Sir, I work for Dr. Jean Formy-Duval"

"I haven't heard of this doctor. Where does he live?"

"I'm here with Dr. Formy-Duval and my father. We are from the Crousilleau Plantation."

"Oh yes, I've heard of Crousilleau. I didn't realize that they were growing such beautiful things there."

"Oh yes, Crousilleau is beautiful, many beautiful flowers there."

The man smiled; she had completely missed his innuendo. "Allow me to introduce myself. I am Pons Durand."

"I am pleased to make your acquaintance," Zoé said, starting to feel a little uncomfortable.

The merchant was holding out the money toward her. She grabbed it, did a quick curtsy, and scampered out the door.

Pons Durand watched her go out the door and to the two men who were probably the doctor and her father. He turned and spoke to the merchant, "I'm going to find out more about that girl."

The merchant smirked and said, "Oh, I'm sure you will. I'm surprised that you don't know all about her or the doctor, working in the port master's office. I would think that they would sell their sugar crops here on the docks of Port-Au-Prince."

"I'm a little surprised too, but the Crousilleau Plantation runs their operation like a cooperative. There are several

171

families involved and I only know Pierre Baptiste Formy. This must be a relative of his."

"Are you going to try to purchase her for your brothel?"

"I would like to. She would be profitable, but maybe more so at my establishment in Martinique. It's been a long time since I've seen a girl with that much beauty and spunk, maybe I could set her up in a house as my mistress; or at least until I get tired of her and then to the brothel."

"Let's go," Zoé said. She had an uneasy feeling as she looked back over her shoulder and saw that man watching her.

That evening Jean found a place to eat that would allow Jules and Zoé to eat together. It was not a very nice place but it did allow both whites and mulattoes to mingle. They had to eat outside on the veranda because of Jules and, even then Jules had to pretend he was a servant-in-waiting. It was nice on the veranda. There was a fine view of the port and harbor and he wanted to reward Zoé for such a good job of selling his merchandise.

The waiter brought their food and even though they were forced to eat outside, they felt like they were dining in fine style. When the waiter brought a small carafe of wine Zoé's eyes lit up. Jean made a mental note to keep an eye on his wine collection back on Crousilleau.

Inside the restaurant, Pons Durand was eating and watching them through an open window. He had assigned a servant to follow them after they had left the apothecary shop. He knew their every move.

Jean walked back inside the restaurant to get the wine carafe refilled. As he approached the bar, Pons Durand, sided up next to Jean and engaged him in a casual and pleasant conversation. After a few casual comments, Pons said, "Tell me about the young slave girl with you."

"That's Zoé. She is a house servant on our plantation."

"I thought so. I knew she was a house slave by the way she spoke and carried herself. She's very beautiful."

All of Belle's fears flashed through Jean's mind and he put himself on guard. "What's your interest in her and who are you?"

"Oh, pardon me. My name is Pons Durand and I'm the assistant port master here in Port-Au-Prince.

Oh damn, thought Jean, *I'll have to be nice to him.*

"Ah, the port master; you must be familiar with our plantation. Crousilleau? We ship all of our sugar through this port," Jean said, hoping that Mr. Durand would know he was a person of some importance and think twice before interfering with his business or his slaves.

It did not seem to faze Pons. He put his proposition to Jean. "I'm interested in purchasing your slave girl, Zoé. That's her name, isn't it?"

"Zoé is not for sale, besides I don't think she would be worth much to you."

"Oh, I think she would be worth a great deal to me at my brothel in Martinique."

Brothel! Jean thought. *I have to finish tomorrow morning and get Zoé back to Crousilleau.*

"I'm sorry, but our family is not interested in selling Zoé. She is a good house servant and a nanny to our children. She cannot be sold."

"I'm sorry to hear that," Pons said, he gave a slight bow, turned and walked out of the restaurant.

By noon the next day, Zoé had sold the remaining medicines and they were leaving Port-Au-Prince.

"Dr. Jean, why do we have to leave so soon? I thought we were going to stay one more night," Zoé asked.

Charles Patton

Jean took a deep breath and said, "Zoé, I didn't want to scare you while we were in Port-Au-Prince, but that man, Pons Durand, wanted to buy you and send you to a brothel in Martinique."

Zoé and Jules recoiled in horror.

"Don't worry, I told him absolutely not. In no case would we sell you, but you can't go back to Port-Au-Prince again. It's too dangerous."

Zoé was quiet for most of the journey to Crousilleau. It was the first time in her life that her slave status had protruded into her life in such a serious manner. As a house servant she had been somewhat sheltered and by living on a prominent plantation she had a life with some means of protection and a quality of life that other slaves did not have. *I could be sold*, she thought. *Now I know why Bando is fighting.*

Bando was tired. Toussaint's army was marching back to a camp in the interior of the island. For three months they had been in constant guerilla warfare with the English, trying to drive them off the island. Toussaint had many successes, but he could not drive the English entirely off the island. He could win in the interior but the English's coastal forts could not be breached.

When the army reached their encampment, Bando was eager to get some rest, but Moyse stuck his head into Bando's tent. "Bando, come to headquarters. Toussaint wants to see his entire staff, including the head sergeants."

Bando groaned and straighten his uniform coat, which was the only part of a uniform that he had, and followed.

Toussaint addressed his staff, "Gentleman, we have come to an agreement with the English."

Bando liked the way Toussaint could say in ten words

174

what took other people a hundred words to say.

Toussaint continued, "The English have agreed to leave our island if I agree *not* to invade Jamaica. Also, I have agreed not to take revenge on the eight thousand black soldiers that the English will leave behind. I expect you to embrace these soldiers and welcome them into our ranks, and of course, I have never had plans to invade Jamaica and I have no intentions of breaking my word to the English. It's a small and easy concession to make to have them leave the island.

"It's now time to turn our attention to the southern part of the island. General Rigaud, the mulatto leader, wants to have the island just for mulattoes and keep the blacks as slaves, or least the ones he hasn't killed yet. In a couple of weeks I'm going to send General Dessalines to the south to defeat him.

Toussaint turned and gave Dessalines a stern look. "I trust you will keep my humane principles with you during your campaign." Dessalines face, as always, showed no emotion but gave his head a slight nod.

Bando knew what Toussaint meant. Both Moyse and Dessalines hated whites, but Dessalines was especially vicious. When he was out from under Toussaint's thumb he could operate without mercy. He had seen Dessalines kill everyone on a plantation, including mulattoes and every black slave. Bando often wondered why Toussaint kept Dessalines on as a general, but down deep he knew why. Anytime there was a particularly difficult and dirty job to be done then Dessalines was the pick. He accomplished the job without regard to how many of his own men's lives he had to spend. He had no regard for human life, neither the enemies, nor his own men.

Toussaint answered a few questions and then dismissed

everyone except Dessalines, Moyse, and surprisingly, Bando.

Toussaint addressed them, "We will have a general planning session tomorrow morning to plan the upcoming southern campaign. "Bando, I want you to leave tomorrow morning for the area around Port-Au-Prince and gather information about General Rigaud and his army. You did say you were from there and familiar with the area?

"Yes sir," Bando said.

"Good, meet with Dessalines when he gets near Port-Au-Prince and tell him what you have found out."

As tired as Bando was, he had a hard time falling asleep that night. This was an important mission and he was proud that Toussaint thought enough of him to assign it to him, but he worried about Dessalines and what he would do once he reached the Crousilleau area. The exciting part was that he would get to see Zoé. He had not visited her in months.

The Intrigues of Napoleon

The day after Bando left for his intelligence mission to the southern part of the island, Toussaint was discussing strategy with Dessalines.

Moyse moved the flap of the tent aside and entered; something he did not usually do unless invited. Toussaint stopped talking, and gave Moyse an agitated look for interrupting him.

"Sir," Moyse said, "another French envoy has arrived. He says he comes straight from Napoleon with direct orders for you."

Toussaint sighed, and motioned to Moyse to let the envoy in. Since Toussaint had ousted the last commissioner, France had quit sending commissioners. They now called them envoys. It was a game played by the French government. Toussaint pretended to be subservient to France and France pretended to be in charge of Toussaint, as demonstrated by the constant stream of envoys with instructions from Napoleon.

A tall gentleman in full French uniform marched into the tent. "Sir, allow me to introduce myself. I am General Hédouville, special agent of Napoleon. May I present my introductory papers?"

"Please, have a seat," Toussaint said, taking the papers and motioning to a chair.

It was quiet for a few moments while Toussaint scanned his papers. They were like all the other introductory papers from French envoys.

Hédouville said, "I have important instructions for you from Napoleon. You are to carry them out immediately." Hédouville handed a packet of papers to Toussaint, and leaned back in his chair to wait.

As Toussaint read the papers he could feel the blood rising to his face and then his eyes almost jumped out of his head. General Hédouville had presented an almost unbelievable set of orders. Toussaint finished and regained his composure. *I have to control my emotions and be diplomatic*, he thought. "This will take some time to digest. Please allow me to discuss this with my staff and we will talk of this again tomorrow."

Hédouville stood, gave a curt bow, and left the tent.

Dessalines and Moyse stayed in the tent as Toussaint read over the instructions again. Finally he looked up at his two best generals.

"What is it?" Moyse asked.

"You won't believe it." He swallowed; Toussaint could barely get the words out. "Napoleon wants me to take our army and invade Jamaica, and then after we take Jamaica, with the additional soldiers we gain there, we are to invade the southern United States."

Moyse and Dessalines sat, wide-eyed and speechless. They had never conceived of such a thing.

After a long pause, Dessalines said, "Are you going to do it?"

"NO! Of course not; it's a trap. This is designed to do two things; one, get me out of Saint-Domingue and give Napoleon full control of Saint-Domingue and, two, to actually invade Jamaica and the southern part of the United States. I can understand Napoleon's devious intentions for the first request, but the invasion of the United States astounds me. I can't imagine what he's thinking."

Toussaint had no way of knowing, but Napoleon had recently and secretly acquired the Louisiana Territory via the *Treaty of Amiens*, this made logical sense to Napoleon that the southeastern part of the United States should adjoin the Louisiana Territory.

"What are you going to do?" Moyse asked.

"Well, I'm *not* leaving Saint-Domingue and, I'm *not* breaking my word to the English about invading Jamaica and, I'm certainly *not* going to invade the United States. The Americans are a very important trading partner and presently a friend in our fight for freedom."

Toussaint rubbed his forehead with his hands and finally shook his head, threw his hands down on the table and said to his two generals, "Let's talk about this tonight. Moyse, send in my secretary. I have to send warning letters to both the British and the Americans."

Back in France Napoleon had every confidence that he could bully Toussaint into invading Jamaica. But he had one worry. If he sent an army to Saint-Domingue to help Toussaint with the Jamaican invasion, then how would the United States react?

Presently, President John Adam's administration was giving their support with full trade and verbal support of Toussaint's policy of freedom for everyone in Saint-Domingue. President Adams was using American warships to help destroy Rigaud's military barges that were menacing the southern coast of Saint-Domingue.

Napoleon would have to wait a year for President Thomas Jefferson to come to power, and then he would be able to attack Saint-Domingue without fear of a negative reaction from the United States.

Toussaint so adamantly disagreed with the plans that he started sending secret messages to both the English and the

United States' ambassadors informing them of Napoleon's plan.

America's Ambassador to Saint-Domingue, Edward Stevens, wrote Secretary of State Pickering, *"I was informed by a black chief* [Toussaint] *...that the Agency of Saint Domingo had received positive Orders from the Executive Directory [France] to invade both the Southern States of America and the Island of Jamaica...*

Before my Departure from Philadelphia I had the Honor of Communicating to you the Intention of the Executive Directory to invade the Island of Jamaica and the southern States of America...the Order of Attack of the former has been renewed and so determined is the French Government on the Invasion that every successive Courier from France has brought out a Copy of the Plan; and the most pressing Solicitations to carry it into immediate Effect...

...Wild and impracticable as the Scheme of Invasion may appear in the actual State of this Colony it is astonishing with what Ardour the Particular Agent seems to urge it...Toussaint on the other hand is determined that the Invasion shall not take Place...

...I have the most perfect Confidence in the Attachment of Toussaint to the Government of the U.S. and in his sincere Desire to establish a beneficial and permanent Commerce between the two Countries...

...Several of our Frigates and Corvettes have been lately here and very kindly received. The Constitution, General Green and Boston are now cruising off the Port...

Every new French envoy who arrived in Saint-Domingue over the next several months pushed the invasion plan to its fullest.

A few months later, after Thomas Jefferson had become the President, France sent an envoy to visit the Jefferson.

Centaur of the Savannahs

Louis André Pichon's purpose was to find out how President Jefferson felt about Toussaint and what would be his reaction to France sending an army to Saint-Domingue to subdue Toussaint.

Pichon called on Jefferson late one afternoon and was ushered into his office where he found Jefferson in a robe and bedroom slippers. Pichon was a little taken back by Jefferson's casual attire but launched into his introductions of himself and his official status as an Envoy of France. They settled down into a casual conversation of current affairs. The conversation soon turned to the Caribbean and Pichon asked Jefferson his opinion of Toussaint. Jefferson was quick to let Pichon know that he did not approve of Toussaint or his project of freedom and independence. Pichon was encouraged by this and followed up with the big question. *"If France were in a position to act, would it not be possible to act, would it not be possible to arrange a concert with the United States in order to accomplish more quickly the conquest of the colony?* And the compromising reply* [from Jefferson] *came: "Without difficulty; but in order that this concert may be complete and effective you must [first] make peace with England; then nothing would be easier than to furnish your army and fleet with everything, and to reduce Toussaint to starvation."*

Pichon pushed a little further and asked the President if there was not favorable opinion in the United States for Toussaint?

Jefferson replied in the negative, *"Was not the negro a menace to two-thirds of the United States? Did not England herself have everything to fear from him? She* [England] *would doubtless participate in a concert to suppress this rebellion, and independently of her fears for her own colonies, I am sure she is observing like us how St.*

181

Domingo is becoming another Algiers in the seas of America."

Jefferson's attitude was typical of a Southern plantation owner. Jefferson's vision for the country was agricultural in outlook, and slave labor, in his opinion, was no problem.

As dismal as this made Jefferson look, in a few weeks he would learn about the secret *Treaty of Amiens,* and how the Louisiana Territory was now in Napoleon's hands. Now the entire picture came clear to Jefferson and why Napoleon needed to have control of Saint-Domingue as a military launching point for Jamaica and the southern United States. He immediately reversed his position on Saint-Domingue and his cozy feelings for Napoleon's France.

ZOÉ

Pons Durant was performing his daily duty of opening the mail for the port master. One of his duties was to open and sort the mail each day in order of importance for the port master to read. Today a letter of low importance had caught his attention. It was from a Claude Sartre, a member of a citizen's committee in France. Pons' eyebrows arched as he read the letter. Apparently, Dr. Formy-Duval was a wanted man back in France.

Pons leaned back in his chair and a plan started forming in his mind. He might be able to use this information to obtain the young slave girl, Zoé. He first thought that he could use the letter as a bargaining chip to force a purchase of Zoé, but on second thought the Formy-Duval family could probably blunt that plan with their family influence. If he kidnapped Zoé, and sent her off to Martinique then at that time he could use it to stop any lawsuits they might pursue. Once the kidnapping was done the courts would be reluctant to take the trouble of making another island government send a slave back to Saint-Domingue. The courts would probably make him pay a steep price for a lost slave; a price he would be more than willing to pay.

If the family persisted then he would threaten exposure of Dr. Formy-Duval to Claude Sartre. Pons put all of the letters on the port master's desk except for the one from Sartre. He then left the port office to find some people that could help him carry out the kidnapping of Zoé.

Later in the afternoon the port master was working his

183

way through the correspondence when he stood up and
went over to Pons' desk, looking for a new ink quill. The
letter from Sartre was lying, face up, on Pons' desk. Since
the letter was addressed to him he picked it up and read it.
He knew who Sartre was seeking. He was well-acquainted
with the Crousilleau Plantation and all the owners. He
picked up Pons' quill, and composed a quick letter to
Sartre, telling him of Dr. Formy-Duval's presence near
Port-Au-Prince.

Jean and company were about halfway back to
Crousilleau when they met a messenger from home. Little
Louis had contracted yellow fever the day they had left and
was now gravely ill.

The family tried everything they knew of to help Louis
during the night. Jean made every medicinal compound he
knew of but Louis died in the early morning hours. Late the
next afternoon they were standing in the family graveyard,
burying little Louis. Jean felt so useless, a doctor who could
not save his own son. He stood next to Jeanne, holding her
shoulder, as she cried. It had progressed rapidly, as it
usually did in children. Belle, Zoé, and Jules were also
there, crying, and helping care for the other children.

This same sorrow affected almost every family that
came to Saint-Domingue. Fifty per cent of all newcomers,
black or white, succumbed to the fever. The remainder
caught the fever but managed to recover, although with
lingering effects for the rest of their lives.

Jeanne contracted yellow fever shortly before she
became pregnant with their last child, but lived through it.
She never regained full strength and the pregnancy with
Alexander had been especially draining on her. She was
becoming frail.

Life was starting to become miserable for Jean and his family: the treacherous flight from France, the fevers and deaths on this island, and most of all the slave revolt which at times seemed poised to wipe out all white colonists on the island. The idea of fleeing the island began to come into a reality more and more. But, where to go? Perhaps another French-held island in the Caribbean, or even, perhaps, New Orleans in the United States.

He had not seen Jeanne have a happy moment or even smile in months. It would be a hard decision to leave their home island largely because of the profits from the plantation. Despite all the outside difficulties they were becoming wealthy. It would be hard to start another plantation somewhere else, but if his families' lives depended on leaving he would not hesitate.

Pons and two other men hid in the forest watching the funeral. Pons pointed out Zoé to the other men, although it was not really necessary. Even in her distressed state, the men could tell this beauty was their target.

Shortly after dark Jules went to his cabin and Zoé followed soon after. Belle, as always, stayed in the main house until late.

The three men crept toward the cabin and then burst in. Zoé screamed. Jules fought as hard as he could but he could not overcome two strong men; Pons held Zoé in a tight grip with one hand over her mouth.

"Run Zoé!" Jules shouted.

Zoé bit Pons' hand and was able to shout, "I can't daddy, I can't get away!"

Everything went blank for Jules, when one of the men hit him over the head with a club.

185

Jean and Belle were in the kitchen talking when Jules stumbled in twenty minutes later, bleeding from the head.

Belle shouted, "Jules, what happened?"

"Dr. Jean, those men from Port-Au-Prince. They done snatched Zoé and took off with her."

Belle screamed, "Oh, my baby!"

"Oh, *mon Dieu*! Jean said. "Belle, we'll get her back. Jules, go tell Master Marc what's happened and to come saddled up, and tell him to bring his pistol."

It took Jules about five minutes to get to the overseer's house. Jacque was incensed that someone would come on his property and steal one of his slaves.

Jean mounted his horse and was adjusting the pistol in his waistband when Marc arrived.

"Which way?" Jacque shouted.

"I'm not sure, but I imagine that they went toward Port-Au-Prince."

Jean and Marc rode their horses hard toward Port-Au-Prince. In about fifteen minutes they started closing in on a carriage and two men on horseback.

"Do you think that's them?" Marc asked.

"It's got to be. There's no one else on the road," Jean replied.

As they closed in, about fifty yards behind the carriage, one of the men on horseback saw them. There was a flurry of activity around the carriage and the men on horseback jumped off and started shooting at them.

Jean and Marc also jumped off their horses and returned fire. It became a standoff and the carriage sped away. Jean stood up to advance toward the two men when a bullet went through his shirt sleeve.

"Jean, Get down. It's not worth it," Marc said.

Jean knew he was right. He would have to pursue it

tomorrow in Port-Au-Prince in a more peaceful manner.

Jean needed a rest. He had been walking around Port-Au-Prince for hours. Of course, no one knew where Pons was, and it was hard to get information about where Pons might be or what property he owned. As assistant port master, people did not want to get on the wrong side of Pons. Word had already spread about what had happened on the Crousilleau Plantation the night before.

Jules was sitting on his bed in his cabin. Belle was inside talking to Jean and Jeanne about his failed efforts to find Zoé. They didn't know what to do. He didn't know what to do either. *People just shouldn't be allowed to steal other people's family,* he thought. All he knew was that he would gladly give up his right to life, if he could get his hands on Durand's throat.

"Jules, Jules," a voice whispered through the window.

Jules, startled, turned and saw Bando standing at the window. "Bando, get in here before someone sees you. You're still a runaway slave you know."

Bando smiled at Jules and asked, "Where's Zoé, is she still in the big house?"

"Sit down, Bando. You're not going to like this."

"What? Has something happened to Zoé?"

"Last week Dr. Jean, Zoé and me went to Port-Au-Prince and while we were there a man named Pons Durand saw Zoé and tried to buy her from Dr. Jean. Of course, Dr. Jean would have nothing to do with it, but Durand and some other men kidnapped her last night and took her to Port-Au-Prince we think."

"What does he think he's going to do with her?" Bando said, his temper rising.

"Dr. Jean says he wants her for his brothel in Martinique.'

"Hell no!" Bando shouted.

"Shhhh, someone will hear you and come put you in irons."

"Is anyone looking for her?"

"Dr. Jean almost got shot last night in a gun battle trying to catch up with her and he spent all day today trying to find her in Port-Au-Prince."

"What do you know about this man, Pons Durand? Bando said, calming down a bit.

"All I know is that he's the assistant port master in Port-Au-Prince, has a brothel there and one in Martinique. Dr. Jean thinks he'll try to ship her to Martinique."

Bando jumped up. "Well, I'm on my way to Port-Au-Prince."

"Be careful, someone will try to put you in irons," Jules said.

"I'm not worried too much about it. I have letters from Toussaint that should keep me out of trouble.'

Jules' eyes widened, "You know Toussaint?"

"I'm on his staff. I work with him almost every day."

Despite his sorrow, Jules almost smiled, he knew someone who knew Toussaint, the great man.

Bando walked the streets and docks of Port-Au-Prince for four weeks. He hung around the docks so he could keep an eye on passengers who boarded any ship. Early each morning, before they went to work, he joined a group of free, black laborers, who worked the docks and discussed all the events of the day. They seemed to know everything that was going on. He sat on edge of the group and tried not to bring attention to himself. The group even discussed the kidnapping of a pretty mulatto slave girl a few times. They alluded that Pons Durand was responsible, but no one said anything that was of any use to him.

Bando found out that Pons had taken a sudden leave-of-absence and no one knew where he was. Bando had broken into Pons' home near the docks and searched for Zoé. He had done the same for every building or warehouse that Pons was known to own or be associated with, but never found any sign of Zoé. No ship had left for Martinique in the last five weeks so he knew that Zoé had not been taken there, yet; although there was a ship scheduled to leave for Martinique in two days.

Bando had concentrated so much on finding Zoé at first that he had felt guilty about not gathering intelligence for Dessalines, but as things turned out, Port-Au-Prince was the best place to find out what was happening all over the region. People arrived every day from all directions to conduct business in Port-Au-Prince. He knew all about Rigaud's army and their present location. He also knew, from refugees, that Dessalines was about ten days away from the Crousilleau Plantation area. He needed to find Zoé soon, get her back to her family, and then get his intelligence information to Dessalines.

This particular morning Bando was at his usual spot, sitting on the edge of the morning discussion group. Seating was important. You did not want to get one of the regular's seat. The topics were the same; ship's arrivals and departures; who was good and bad to work for; where to get the best food and so on. Bando was sitting there, half listening and watching a ship being docked, where he heard, "Did they ever find that little slave girl that Pons stole?"

"No, I don't think so; don't know where Pons could

have stashed her," one of the group said.

There was a moment of reflection and one old-timer spoke up and said, "If I remember right, I took some packages to that big two-story house on the east end of town one time. The one near the beach, and I'm sure I saw Pons there. I wonder if that's where he's keeping her. He acted like he owned the place."

The rest of the group shrugged it off but that was enough for Bando. He knew the house; it was prominent and lavishly decorated. He would check it out this afternoon and break-in tonight.

Bando spent all afternoon observing what had to be the house the laborers had talked about that morning. It was right on the beach. He picked out a secluded spot where he could observe the house without anyone noticing him. It was dusk and he was watching the remaining colors of the sunset. He had never seen or could have imagined such luxury before leaving Crousilleau. In his service to Toussaint, on the Northern Plains, he had seen many plantation houses that were luxurious, but this house had a beautiful view of the ocean and the sunset every night. It was hard to fathom that some people lived in such beauty and luxury. *Maybe the revolt will allow me to have something nice someday*, he thought.

A shuttered window was being opened on the top floor of the house that he was watching. All afternoon every window had been open except for one room. A middle-aged mulatto lady seemed to be airing it out. He could see her moving around in the room as if she was straightening it. About ten minutes later she closed the shutters.

That has to be where she is, Bando thought. It was a perfect spot. A dingy was beached on the shore in front of the house. Pons could have someone put Zoé in the rowboat, and row about a mile to the west where the ships were anchored, and put her on a ship to Martinique. No one would ever see her on the docks, especially if they did it after dark.

So what's my plan, he wondered. He looked over his shoulder at his horse. It was tied nearby, ready for their escape. *I can't just knock on the front door, rush in, and grab her.* He had seen two men about the house all afternoon. They looked like guards. One of them came out of the house, mounted a horse and left riding toward town. *Good, one less guard. Now's the time.* He decided to climb the trellis that led up to a second floor window that was open. He got his sword that he kept hidden in his bedroll, and crept toward the house and up the trellis.

Bando peered into the second floor window. He was at the end of a long hall. There was a guard that appeared to be half-asleep, sitting in a chair, near the door of a room at the far end of a hall. Bando was halfway down the hall when a muffled scream was heard from behind the door. The guard opened his eyes, shifted his body and spotted Bando approaching. The guard jumped up and raised his sword to engage Bando.

Bando smiled to himself. This was child's play. He had been in more than fifty sword fights in the last year; all life and death situations. He had killed every opponent due to his training by the ex-French military officer. Bando parried the first blow, countered with a blow that knocked the sword out of the guard's hand, and killed him by running him through. It had taken barely ten seconds, but there had been enough noise to alert someone inside the door.

The door opened about six inches and a man took a quick look through the opening. Bando knew it had to be

Pons Durand. Bando kicked it open, sending Pons across the room and he landed against a chair.

Bando sized up the room and situation in a couple of seconds. Zoé was tied by each hand to a bedpost. Her eyes were wide-open and she was trying to scream from behind a gag.

Bando rushed Pons immediately. Bando's experience had taught him not to give his opponent any time to think or compose themselves. Engage and kill.

"Who the hell are you!" Pons screamed. He could see the dead guard out in the hall.

"I'm your last memory," Bando said as he charged Pons.

Their swords locked and then went through a series of parries. After a minute of hard fighting, Bando thought to himself, *This man's had training. I've never had a sword fight last longer than a few parries.*

They were locked, sword to sword, about six inches from each other when Bando kicked Pons backwards with his foot. Pons charged again. As Pons started toward him, Bando reached down to a desk and grabbed an inkwell and threw it in Pons' face. This startled Pons for a second. It was just enough time for Bando to step forward and give one mighty sweep of his sword that knocked Pons' weapon to the floor. Bando grabbed Pons and spun him around. Bando dropped his sword and snatched a knife out of his waistband. He now had one hand across Pons' chest and his other hand held the knife against Pons' throat.

Zoé struggled through the entire fight and managed to slip her gag enough to talk.

"Bando, oh, thank God!"

"Has he hurt you?" Bando asked, fearing the answer.

Zoé teared up and cried out, "He raped me!"

Bando did not hesitate. Within a second of her reply he

slit Pons' throat and pushed him to the floor. Pons thrashed around for a few seconds and then bled out and died.

Bando freed Zoé, grabbed her hand, and led her down the stairs. Zoé could hardly walk but she managed by leaning on Bando. At the bottom of the stairs the mulatto woman stood with her hands over her mouth.

Bando brought up his sword and said, "Say anything and I'll come back and kill you." She could only nod her head and back away.

Zoé began getting some leg strength back and was able to run with Bando toward his horse. As they neared the horse she started feeling faint and fell down.

"I have to rest a minute."

Bando reached into a saddlebag and pulled out some bread and wine. "Hear, have some of this." Zoé devoured the bread and gulped the wine.

"Didn't they feed you?"

"I was on a hunger strike. I don't think I could have lasted much longer."

"Well, put the wine away. You can chew on the bread while we ride. We've got about ten or fifteen minutes before that woman screams her bloody head off."

"Bloody head? You didn't touch her."

Bando shook his head and smiled, "Never mind. I've just picked up too much slang from being around English prisoners."

Bando and Zoé arrived at the Crousilleau Plantation about midnight. They tied up the horse in the woods and then walked toward Belle's cabin.

"Oh, my baby," screamed Belle.

"Shhh, momma, you'll wake up everyone. Bando can't be seen here."

Belle and Jules hugged and kissed Zoé for a minute while Bando sat down on the bed to rest. It had been a long, nerve-racking day and he was worn out.

After a few minutes Belle came over and started thanked Bando. Bando interrupted her and said, "You can't tell anyone how I rescued her or even that I was here. Tell anyone who asks that Zoé escaped and ran home on her own. They may not believe you, but that's what you say."

Zoé walked Bando back to his horse, kissed him goodbye and said, "When will I see you again?"

"Soon, I hope. I'm not sure. I have to find Dessalines and tell him the location of Rigaud's army."

Dessalines Marches South

Dessalines' march south was one of the bloodiest campaigns under the Toussaint banner. There was no mercy given at any point. Whites, mulattoes, and blacks were killed indiscriminately. So horrific was Dessalines' campaign of cruelty that when Toussaint later learned of the facts, he covered his face with his hands and cried out, *"I told him to prune the bush, not uproot it!"*

The Crousilleau Plantation was in a state of panic. The family elders were gathered on the veranda of Jean Baptiste's home. The argument had been going on for half an hour.

"We should all band together. I can raise an army from this area to defend our plantations," Jean Baptiste said, raising his voice.

"How are you going to defend against five or ten thousand black soldiers, especially Dessalines' type?" said Dr. Jean.

"What do you suggest, run?" said Jean Baptiste.

"Yes, take the money we have and leave," said Dr. Jean.

"Maybe we could move to Port-Au-Prince temporarily and join others there. I think Port-Au-Prince can be defended," Uncle Ores said.

"Possibly," said Jean, "but I am not going to risk my family on the possibility of defending Port-Au-Prince."

"Well, do what you think is best for your family. We are going to fight for our homes," said Jean Baptiste.

Jean walked a few hundred yards to his own home, thinking how he was going to tell Jeanne that once again they had to flee. First from France and now Saint-Domingue.

He had to get his family out of here, even though Jeanne's health had become frail since Alexander's birth.

Jeanne knew there was something on Jean's mind as soon as he walked in the door. They had been having discussions for days now about the black army that was coming their way, but tonight his face was different. He was not puzzled or perturbed. He looked like a man who had made up his mind.

"Jeanne, sit down; I must talk to you," Jean said.

"Yes *cheri*, what is it?" she replied.

"Jeanne, we have to get out of Saint-Domingue. We have to leave if we are to escape with our lives and the children to have a future," Jean said.

Jeanne's reply surprised Jean, "Yes, I agree we must leave. We have to leave for our children's sake and our own. I have been ready to leave for months now. Make the arrangements."

"Are you sure you can make a sea voyage? You seem so frail."

"Either die at the hands of a marauding black army or die at sea. There's no choice, we have to go," Jeanne said.

"I'll go into Port-Au-Prince tomorrow to see if I can book some sort of passage for us. I have no idea what the destination will be. I'll try for another French island but we may have to take what's available," Jean said.

It took Jean most of the day to reach Port-Au-Prince and the dock area of the port. He was disappointed by the number of ships in the harbor. Usually fifteen or twenty ships were always in port, but President Jefferson's new administration was trying to starve commerce with Saint-Domingue. Most of the ships were traveling to other parts of the island. Only one ship, the *Nellie*, was leaving the island. It was going to the Carolinas. Jean thought to himself, *Maybe they could go somewhere else from the Carolinas.*

Jean walked up the gangplank of the *Nellie* and asked the nearest crewman for the captain. The crewman went below to find the captain and told him that they had a visitor. In a few moments a tall, bearded man came on deck and walked toward Jean.

"I am Captain Chaffe. What can I do for you?" he said.

"My name is Dr. Jean Formy-Duval, and I am looking for passage off this island for myself and my family."

"Had enough of the black army, huh?," he said.

"Yes, I must get my family to safety", Jean replied.

"Well, I have bad news for you. You are going to find that only a few American merchant ships will take on passengers. If we do that and the black leaders find out about it, then they may not let us do business here anymore. Toussaint wants the white colonists to stay and run their plantations," he explained.

"Yes, and while we stay here his other generals are killing us," Jean said with a touch of sarcasm.

"All the same, my owners do not want to make enemies here," the captain said.

Jean signed, nodded his acknowledgement by tipping his hat, and walked down the gangplank. What more could he do? He would have to find a more accommodating ship.

On the way home he had several encounters on the road with other planters and was alarmed at their information on Dessalines' army and how close he was. He began formulating an alternative plan in case he had not booked passage by the time Dessalines' army arrived.

Arriving at Crousilleau, he greeted Jeanne and told her of the events of the day and then went to find Jules.

Jules was working in the garden. He was working with a tree that had been imported from Asia and fascinated him. This tree grew about fifteen or twenty feet tall and had pink, or sometimes, purple blooms at the ends of the branches. The leaves looked like the leaves of the myrtle tree and the leaf texture was like crepe paper, so the common name that he had always heard was Crepe Myrtle.

"Jules," called out Jean when he entered the garden.

"Yes sir," Jules replied, turning his attention away from the tree.

"We have a problem coming our way. Dessaline's army is a few days away and my family must get out of here," Jean said.

Jean paused and then continued, "I need for you to go to our fishing boat at the beach and get it ready. Provision it as if eight or ten people were going to be out fishing for two or three days. Also, take one of our most trusted field hands and have him guard it over the next few days. If Dessaline gets here before I can work things out, then we may have to make a run for it."

Jules took this in and said, "That Dessalines is killing all the house slaves and mulattoes as he goes along. Is there room for Belle, Zoé, and me?"

"I think so, but I'm not sure," Jean said, while thinking that he probably could not book passage on a ship for them, but he could take them in the family fishing boat if they had to go to sea.

Centaur of the Savannahs

A few weeks earlier in France, Claude Sartre had an unexpected audience with none other than Napoleon Bonaparte himself. Sartre had, for years, been trying to find out what had happened to Dr. Jean Formy-Duval and his family. Sartre was well known in the government circles for his ardor in finding enemies of the state. He had recently received information from a source in Port-Au-Prince that indicated that Dr. Formy-Duval was in that area. Lately, Sartre had been hounding officials to send him on a mission to apprehend the doctor.

The summons for him to come to General Bonaparte's office was highly unusual and made him a little more than apprehensive. Had he done something wrong? What could the general possibly want with him?

A young officer escorted him into the general's office and the general motioned for him to take a seat across from his desk.

Napoleon started the conversation and went straight to the point, asking, "Are you the official that Robespierre used to find enemies of the state?"

"Yes, I am," Sartre said uneasily.

"Were you the one sent to find Dr. Formy-Duval?," Napoleon asked.

"Yes, but he eluded me. I thought he went to Canada, but I never found him. Sir, recently I have received information that suggests that he is in Saint-Domingue near Port-Au-Prince."

Napoleon digested the information for a moment, an eternity for Sartre who thought he was in some kind of trouble. Napoleon continued and spoke with considerable agitation, "This is the same medical doctor who faked an execution that I presided over when I was a young captain. It could have gotten me in a great deal of trouble. It was the only time in my career that someone has tricked me in such a manner and gotten away with it."

Sartre's anxiety relaxed a little. This could go his way. Napoleon continued, "I am going to give you letters that will allow you to go anywhere in the Caribbean or the Americas on ships of French registry. Bring him back here if you can, so I can enjoy his execution. If you cannot extradite him then carry out French justice where ever you find him and I mean extreme justice. Do you understand what I mean?"

Sartre smiled and said, "Do not worry my General, I will either find him and bring him back to you or carry out French justice where ever I find him."

"Good, there's a fast military frigate leaving tomorrow for Saint-Domingue. Be on it and you should be there soon," Napoleon said, looking down at his paperwork and waving Sartre off.

"O Purple beauty of old lands
And days beyond the sunrise sea,
That thou art here in alien hands-
What tricks hath Fortune played on thee?"
Kinchen Council
A Crepe Myrtle Reverie

Book Three

THE CAROLINAS

Escape To the Sea

Bando's horse was becoming tired as it moved through the dense brush that grew on this part of the island. Daily rain had made it especially thick. Bando was desperate to reach the Crousilleau Plantation.

Two days ago he had located Dessalines' camp. Dessalines was drunk and in a foul mood. He was unhappy that Bando was so late in bringing the information he needed. Bando actually feared for his life, but Dessalines calmed down after he heard Bando's intelligence report. It was what he needed to know to find Rigaud's army.

It was late afternoon and Bando told some of Dessalines' staff that he was riding out to scout the area, but in truth, he was on the way to Crousilleau again.

There was an advance detachment of Dessalines' army heading toward Crousilleau, intent on destroying the plantations in that area. Bando was only thirty minutes to an hour ahead of them. He had to get to Zoé and get her away from the plantation. Not only were they killing all the whites, but also any mulattoes or house servants that they could find. House servants were considered to be too closely attached to the white planters.

Bando left his horse in the woods about a mile from Crousilleau. He ran the rest of the way and fell to his knees in exhaustion fifty yards from Zoé's cabin. He allowed himself about thirty seconds to catch his breath and then crept up to the only window on their cabin. He looked inside and saw Zoé and Belle asleep. Jules was sitting by the remains of the light of a cooking fire. He was tying a small sapling tree, about eighteen inches in length, with dirt and burlap.

"Jules," Bando whispered.

"Bando," Jules said.

Zoé and Belle, startled, woke up. Zoé rushed to the window and threw her arms around Bando's neck. "What are you doing here?" she cried out. "Don't stay out there. Someone will see you. Come inside."

Bando rushed inside and warned them. "Zoé, you must leave with me. Dessalines' army could be here within the hour. I can only take you with me."

"I cannot leave my mother!"

"Zoé, you must come with me, and your mother and Jules must flee to Port-Au-Prince for safety."

"No, I must see my mother to safety!"

Jules stepped forward and asked Bando, "Will they kill us blacks?"

"Not all. They will Zoé, because she is a mulatto and you two because you will be considered house servants."

"I have to warn the Doctor and his wife", Belle said as she went out the door.

"No," shouted Bando, knowing that this was getting out of hand. He was not here to save whites but he let Belle go.

Belle ran to the house, in the back door, and was halfway up the stairs leading to the bedrooms, shouting "Doctor Jean! Doctor! Wake up!"

Jean opened their door, looking disheveled and alarmed. "What is it Belle?"

"Dessalines' men... they'll be here within the hour!"

It took Jean a couple of seconds to digest what she said and all the implications. He ran to the end of the hall where a window looked out to the plantation grounds. The sky to the east and north was bright with what was surely burning plantation houses and sugar fields.

He turned and shouted to Belle, "Tell Jules to get the wagon ready to take us to the boat."

Belle pleaded with her eyes and said, "What about us?"

Jean understood. "You and Jules and Zoé can come too, but hurry! We have to get to the boat."

Jeanne had been listening at the door and knew what she had to do. She had already packed two trunks with essential clothing and items. They had also taken the precaution of gathering money, almost all of it in gold, which they had saved since being on the plantation. She had put it in a type of sock about ten inches long. The sock had strings at the top and bottom so that it could be tied to her neck and around her waist. The sock itself rested between her breasts. Not many people had the nerve to body search a plantation owner's wife. Jean also threw in French land deeds and other documents relating to their property and financial holdings in Saint-Domingue and France.

Jean dragged the two trunks down the stairs and out onto the veranda while Jeanne dressed the three children.

Jules had the wagon brought to the veranda and in a few

minutes and they loaded the trunks on the wagon. Jules, Belle and Zoé had nothing to pack. They only owned what they wore. Jean did notice that Jules threw in a stick of some sort but did not have time to ask about it.

As they were loading everyone he noticed that the slaves were coming outside and looking at the sky to the east. It was bright with fire and cinders. They knew what was coming, their freedom. Many started shouting and dancing. Jean gave the horses a tap with the whip and drove the wagon off the plantation, the horses at a run.

As they left the plantation grounds, Jeanne looked at it one last time. Her last glimpse, which would stay in her mind for the rest of her life, was toward the family graveyard where little Louis was buried.

As soon as Jean drove the wagon onto the trail to the beach, three miles away, he looked around in the wagon and saw Bando in the back.

"What the hell is he doing here?" Jean shouted.

"Dr. Jean, he is the one that warned us," Belle said.

Jean looked at Bando and said, "I thought you were with Toussaint?"

"I am, but I had to warn about Dessalines' men," Bando said. What he didn't say was that he only came to save Zoé and no one else. He was not quite sure what he was doing in the wagon except trying to get Zoé to come with him once her mother was onboard the boat and safely out to sea.

Jean thought for a minute. It didn't quite make sense but he accepted it. He did not have time to do anything else.

On Crousilleau, Dessalines' men reached the plantation and become so engrossed in looting, plundering and burning that the other members of the Crousilleau Clan managed to get away toward Port-Au-Prince. Soon a mounted black officer came upon the scene at Crousilleau and started asking questions about the owners. He was told about a wagon load of whites heading off on the road toward the beach.

The officer organized a pursuit party and headed after them.

Jean had exhausted the horses but they made it to the beach in about thirty minutes. The slave guarding the boat helped them load the trunks and children. The boat was designed for a fishing party of about ten to fifteen people plus gear. About halfway through the loading two other white families ran down to their location. How they found out about their boat and plans Jean did not know but they were pleading to be put in the boat. They were the De Rossetts and Cluveires, both with children. Jean could not refuse them. He had room, but barely.

Zoé was the last person to get in the boat. She was afraid to upset Bando too soon.

Bando spotted her as she climbed in and shouted, "Zoé, what are you doing? I thought you were coming with me."

"Bando, I can't leave my mother until I know she is safe. Come with us," she pleaded.

"I cannot. I'm a soldier serving on Toussaint's staff. I cannot desert!"

The men were now pushing off the boat from the beach and Bando was getting desperate. "What port are you going to?" he shouted.

"I don't know but come find me," Zoé pleaded.

"But where?" Bando shouted.

Jeanne was watching Zoé and took pity on her and leaned over the boat rail and said to Bando, "We don't know but possibly the Carolinas."

Bando helped push the boat off as he heard distant hoof beats coming toward them. He and the assisting slave sprinted for the dense foliage near the beach and hid. Moments later the black assault group rushed onto the beach. The officer had the only gun and fired it at the boat which was about thirty yards out past the breakers. The shot nicked the boat's railing and ricocheted into the water.

"Come find me!" Bando heard Zoé crying out over and over.

Jean rigged a small sail with the intent of trying to `position the boat in the sea lane that left Port-Au-Prince. It took until noon the next day to get to where Jean thought that they might be in the sea lane out of Port-Au-Prince. Most everyone had been seasick but they were over it now and most were sleeping as best they could. Jean's main worry was water. There were more people on board than he had anticipated. He had enough food for several days but the water would run out soon.

The rest of the day went by without seeing a ship. Jean raised the sail every now and then to adjust their position. He needed to stay in the sea lane but just out of sight of Port-Au-Prince. Every four hours he headed for land to see if he could see the Port-Au-Prince area and get his bearings. As soon as he ascertained where they were, he headed out so no one from Port-Au-Prince could see him.

By the afternoon of the next day they only had a few drops of water left. They would give it to the children.

Jean was looking over his passengers when he saw Jules eyes fasten on to something and raise half way out of his seat. Jean looked in the direction that Jules was staring. There on the horizon, sailing out of Port-Au-Prince, was a merchant ship coming their way. Everyone's spirits picked up and they started waving rags to get the ship's attention.

When the ship spotted them, it turned in their direction.

As it came closer, Jean's heart dropped. It was Captain Chaffe's ship, the *Nellie*.

The ship pulled alongside and threw over a rope. Jean grabbed one so they would not separate from the ship.

Captain Chaffe looked over the side of his ship. He and Jean locked eyes. Captain Chaffe spoke first, "I heard about the trouble in your area."

"Yes Captain, that's why we're here, at your mercy."

There was a long silence and Captain Chaffe's mind was battling between duty and compassion.

Jeanne spoke up, "Please Captain, look at these children; surely you will rescue us and not let them die."

Captain Chaffe gave in. He was far enough away so that no one from Port-Au-Prince could see them and his conscience would not let him leave them to the mercy of the sea.

"All right, come on aboard. I'll take you to the Carolinas; hope you like swamps and pine trees. Men, help these people aboard," the Captain shouted.

The children were the first taken aboard. Jeanne was next but almost lost her balance because of all the gold coins strapped to her chest. Jean grabbed her from behind, steadied her, and helped her up the rope ladder. The rest came aboard without incident and the group was given quarters in the cargo hold. Jean was grateful for even that, seeing that this was a cargo ship and there was nothing better available.

Jean and Captain Chaffe negotiated a group fare for everyone in his party. The Captain said he would only charge for what he thought would be expenses for food and drink. Jean paid him with a couple of gold coins.

"Where are we headed?" Jean asked.

"Georgetown, South Carolina is the first stop and then on to Smithville, North Carolina and then up the Cape Fear

River to Wilmington. Then we head back to Port-Au-Prince," the Captain answered.

Do you know what areas would be good for French Colonists to be welcomed?" Jean asked.

The Captain thought for a moment and then said, "Dr. Formy-Duval, you may find that your arrival may not be too friendly. Since the slave revolt started about eight or nine years ago there have been ten to twenty thousand French immigrants to the coasts of the United States, most from Saint-Domingue. That is one of the main reasons why the *Alien and Sedition Act* was passed by Congress, to try to ship the French back to France. You may want to try passing for another nationality or keep a low profile for a while until you decide what is best for you."

"Is it as bad as that? I had heard the United States wanted immigrants," Jean said.

"They do, but the people of the United States are of English descent and you know how the French and English have fought for the last century. But don't despair; it is not as bad as all that, especially since Thomas Jefferson has become President. His sympathies lie with the French and he would like to repeal the *Alien and Sedition Act*. Live quietly and don't agitate people. Most Americans will accept you if you are honest, willing to help each other and have a pleasing personality."

"Do we have to get off at the first port?"

"No," the Captain replied, "you can choose any one of the three ports, but if you haven't chosen by the time we get to Wilmington, then you will have to get off there."

"Fair enough," Jean said.

Claude Sartre was searching the streets of Port-Au-Prince for any information concerning Dr. Formy-Duval.

Many people knew of him and his extended family. Sartre had found out about his plantation at Crousilleau and traveled there to gather information but it was scarce because most people on the plantation were gone. He did manage to find out that they had fled in a fishing boat.

Bando, now with a small military detachment in Port-Au-Prince, had become aware of Sartre's search for Dr. Formy-Duval. He was discretely following him on the docks, trying to find out any information that would also tell him where Dr. Formy-Duval and Zoé might have headed.

By listening, he heard Sartre determine the date that the Formy-Duvals fled in their fishing boat, determine which merchant ships left during that time frame and finally deduce that if they didn't drown at sea, then they had to be on the *Nellie*, headed for the Carolinas.

Bando was impressed. If he quit Dessalines' command and somehow attached himself to this man, then he might find Zoé. Although he had great admiration for Toussaint, he had become sickened with Dessalines' cruelty and had come to realize that he should have gone with Zoé.

Over the next couple of days Bando managed to have conversations with Sartre. Bando's knowledge of the Formy-Duvals and his willingness to attach himself to Sartre as a type of valet for him led Sartre to invite Bando to travel with him. Bando was not fond of the deal but Sartre just might find the Formy-Duvals and he could put up with Sartre until then, if it meant finding Zoé.

Sartre soon found a French merchant ship going to the Carolinas and showed the ship's captain his letter from Napoleon. They were given free passage for the voyage.

Charles Patton

Here's to the land of the cotton bloom white, Where the scuppernong perfumes the breeze at night,   Where the soft southern moss and Jessamine mate, 'Neath the murmuring pines of the Old North State!

<u>The North Carolina State Toast</u>, 2nd Verse

The Riverfront At Wilmington

Jean and Jeanne leaned against the rail of the *Nellie*. They were looking at the small river city and port of Wilmington, North Carolina.

Wilmington was not actually on the coast but was up an ocean inlet formed by the Cape Fear River. You had to navigate the dangerous Cape Fear shoals, which lead into the river and then travel about twenty-five miles to reach the docks at Wilmington.

The entire traveling party had decided against Georgetown, South Carolina. They had taken a quick tour of Georgetown and had decided against it, because of all the plantations and rice fields that depended on slave labor. It reminded them too much of Saint-Domingue. While they were there, Captain Chaffe unloaded their fishing boat which he had lashed to the deck of his ship. Jean could come back for it later or even sell it there.

The next stop, at the entrance of the Cape Fear River, had been Smithville. After a short tour they decided it was too small. It was a small harbor town that provided river pilots to large ships traveling up the river. There was no opportunity there.

Now at the Wilmington riverfront, all the families left

210

the boat and headed up the small hill to a combined business and residential section. They had rented a driver who had a horse and small wagon to carry their luggage. The driver followed the families including Jules, Belle and Zoé. The children thought it was great fun to ride in the wagon.

They had gone no further than a block when Mr. De Rosset suddenly stopped. His eyes were fixed on a sign above a door opening. It said *Dr. Armond de Rosset, Doctor.*

"I'm supposed to have some relatives somewhere here in the Carolinas. I wonder if this is one of them?" De Rosset said.

Jean said, "You and your wife go on in and find out; we will wait here and rest."

Jean watched through the window and observed as a casual conversation started and then both parties became more excited and then erupting into outright embraces and celebrations.

Mr. De Rosset rushed back outside and said that this was a distant cousin whom he had not seen since a small child and that all were invited to their place until everyone could get settled.

The next couple of weeks provided a welcome rest for everyone, especially Jeanne. She had become even paler and weaker than before. Jean was worried about her but could do nothing but encourage her to rest and relax.

Within a week Jean found a small house near the dock area and moved his family into it. The De Rossets and Cluveires stayed at the De Rosset plantation but both families were having a difficult time adjusting. They had experienced a very narrow escape, having even less time to escape their plantations in Saint-Domingue than the Formy-

211

Duvals. They had actually seen Dessalines' soldiers come on their plantation and kill people. They barely had time to grab their children by the hand and run desperately through the woods toward the beach hoping to find an escape of any kind.

They found the De Rosset's plantation, complete with slavery, uncomfortable to live with. They were becoming paranoid of black people even though the blacks on the plantation treated them with kindness.

Jean had been worried about how additional French immigrant families would be welcomed here. There was only minor or no resentment by most, but some people were adamant about carrying out the *Alien Removal Act*. As it turned out, he found that if he did like Captain Chaffe advised, and kept a low profile, then most people were friendly and accommodating.

One evening Jean was talking to Jeanne about their prospects and asked Jeanne how she felt about the Wilmington area as an area of potential settlement. She replied, "I like the climate, it is a little cooler than Saint-Domingue, and other French families seem to be doing well here. I do not see why we couldn't do the same."

"I think you may be right. I went to a land speculator's office today. There is land along the Cape Fear River, a few miles up from Wilmington, where we could start a plantation. It is fairly expensive though. Now, as another option, the further inland you go from Wilmington, the cheaper the land is. I saw one large parcel of land south of a lake call Waccamaw that is being sold by the heirs of the Patrick Henry family, of Virginia. It can be bought cheap," Jean said.

"Where is this lake?" Jeanne asked.

"It is about thirty-five mile inland from here. There are

two ways to get there. One is to go to Elizabeth town and then take an old Indian road. That's the quickest if you are walking or by horseback. If you have baggage and a family, then it is probably best to go back to Georgetown and take a boat up the Waccamaw River towards the lake," Jean answered.

"Does that parcel of land include the lake?"

"No, the northern edge of it is just south of the lake."

"Which do you prefer?" Jeanne asked.

"I think I would rather spend the extra money on land for an existing plantation near Wilmington. That would make it easier for us to take crops to Wilmington and sell them along the docks for export to Europe; socially it would be easier for us. Also, there would be schools here for the children,"

Jeanne thought for a moment and then said, "The main thing I want is for our family to be safe. I trust your judgment. Do what you think is best." She was tiring and wanted to rest.

The next day Jean was at the land speculator's office talking about different properties that were for sale along the Cape Fear River. The speculator tried to steer Jean inland toward the cheaper property near Lake Waccamaw. It had been for sale for several months now with no interest, largely because much of it was swamp land. He had been promised a higher commission rate than normal if he could sell it, but Jean seemed to have little interest in it. Jean had thought about the property but would only consider it if things become too dangerous for French immigrants. If it came to that then he and his family could live there without bother from anyone. Settlers in the interior pretty much lived by their own rules and means.

As they talked about properties, they sat at a table in

front of a large window that looked over the riverfront. It was a nice view and it was interesting to watch the activity on the docks and all the people as they walked by the window. There was a plantation on the Cape Fear River for sale that Jean was interested in, and they were doing the initial stages of negotiation, an intriguing and slow verbal dance, so to speak, when Jean stiffened. He thought he saw a familiar figure walking up the street.

He walked over to the edge of the window, keeping himself hidden. It was Sartre and Bando. He knew who they were looking for, Sartre for him and Bando to find Zoé. They were working together.

Sartre did not have the authority to arrest him here so he would probably try to kill him. It had been years since he had fled France, why was the French Directorate so persistent in their pursuit?

His families' fortunes had turned in an instance. Now he knew he would have to settle in the interior of the state. If one secret envoy assassin could not do the job then they would send another one. Somehow, they had tracked him to Wilmington. He had to flee inland.

He turned to the speculator and made an immediate deal for the large parcel of land below Lake Waccamaw. Much of it was swamp land but high places could occasionally be found, enough for a farm or small plantation, plus the Waccamaw River ran through the middle of it and he could ship his crops to Georgetown for export. Jean made his way home, checking at every street crossing for Sartre and Bando before proceeding. It was late afternoon when he rushed in to find Jeanne.

"Jeanne, Sartre is here in Wilmington and Bando is with him!"

"*O mon Dieu*, what are we going to do?" she cried.

"We have to leave at first light tomorrow morning. I have arranged for a horse and wagon to pick us up and take us to the wharf where a small ship leaves for Smithville every morning," Jean said.

"What ship?"

"It's a ship that takes harbor pilots back to Smithville after they have guided vessels past all the dangerous shoals and on to the Wilmington docks."

"What will we do in Smithville?" Jeanne asked.

"Catch another boat to Georgetown. Then take our own boat into Winyah Bay and up the Waccamaw River to our land."

Jean spent the next hour talking with Jeanne about the land they had bought and his reasons why he had bought it. Again she replied, "I don't care, as long as you can get us to someplace safe."

Jean said some quick goodbyes that evening to the few friends they had made but left their destination vague. When he talked to the De Rossets and Cluveires, they begged Jean to take them with him. He agreed after realizing the depths of their traumatization and fears. He was also thinking that it might take more than one family to make things work on the isolated land that he had purchased.

The next morning he had his family, including Jules, Belle, Zoé, the two other families and assorted baggage on board the small ship headed toward Smithville.

They arrived at Smithville about mid-afternoon and Jean managed to find a place to board everyone including Jules and his family, although they had to sleep in slave quarters.

After everyone was settled, he walked down to the port and began asking about passage to Georgetown. It wasn't difficult because it was the next coastal town south of them.

215

The captain of a small merchant vessel agreed on a price for Jean and his entourage. They would leave at high tide the next morning.

Jeanne had to put her arm on Jean's shoulder as they walked down to the dock the next morning. She was weak and needed someone to hold her arm in order to make it onto the ship. Jean helped her up the gangplank and she collapsed on a bench on deck. Jean was beginning to become more worried about her. She was getting weaker and weaker, but she insisted on making the trip if it meant safety for her family.

She realized that if Jean were killed, then who would take care of a sick widow with three children? Her children could possibly become orphans in this uncivilized foreign land. Safety for Jean meant safety for her family.

The journey to Georgetown was a welcome relief. It was July and the Carolina weather was hot but sailing off the coast provided a constant breeze which was far better than sweltering on land. It was a day and a half trip and they arrived the next day in the early afternoon.

They made their way to their fishing boat and decided to stay with it for a couple of days while they provisioned themselves for the journey to their settlement. They made camp near the edge of the woods. It was better than finding accommodations in Georgetown. The sea breeze was much more comfortable than being cooped up in an old boarding house in town.

Jean and Jules walked into town and went about the business of buying provisions not only for the voyage up the Waccamaw River but also all the tools necessary when starting a new homestead; tools, nails, firearms, powder and numerous other items. The general store where they had bought most of the merchandise used its own driver and wagon to deliver everything to the dock.

Jean also found two young river men who knew all of the five rivers that fed into a big bay named Winyah. They said they had made numerous trips up the Waccamaw River and were familiar with it. After examining Jean's boat to determine if the draft was shallow enough to make it up the river, they agreed to Jean's proposal.

They would not only navigate but they would pole the boat upstream against the light current. They would tie a small canoe to the back of Jean's boat so that they could return home. They would return in half the time it would take them to get to Jean's land because the canoe was light and paddling with the current they could make a quick trip back to Georgetown. They agreed to start the next morning and expected the trip to take four or five days if everything went well.

That evening, Jean and Jules were packing the boat, when again, Jean saw Jules throw in that stick tied up with burlap.

"Jules, I have been meaning to ask you; what is that stick you have been carrying this whole trip?" Jean asked.

Jules smiled and said, "Dr. Jean, this is my myrtle tree. You know, it's the one with all the pretty purple flowers that bloom on the end of the branches."

"Oh yes, the one from Asia. So you brought the purple one instead of the pink one. Some people call it a Crepe Myrtle," Jean said.

"Dr. Jean, you know I like plants and such. I wanted to bring something to remind me of home, you know, Crousilleau."

"That's a great idea, Jules. We will plant it and from its seeds we can plant the whole plantation with myrtles, to remind us of Crousilleau. Since the land is supposed to be high land by the river and the back area cut off by swamps it will be our own garden place where no one can find us," Jean exclaimed.

The Waccamaw River

The next morning the two young men arrived ready to start the trip. Jean showed the men a surveyor's map of the land he had purchased. They recognized the area on the map because of their numerous trips to Lake Waccamaw. They had taken several hunting and fishing parties there. They pointed out what they called a high ridge in the swamp, where they indicated might be the best place to settle.

The first few hours of the trip, where they could use the sail, went smoothly across Winyah Bay, but as soon as they entered the Waccamaw River the wind ceased to help them, because of the dense foliage on both sides of the river. Here the two young men started earning their money as pole men.

The next five days was like nothing they had ever seen. You could either be scared to death of the landscape or find it fascinating. The cypress trees lining the riverbanks were covered with Spanish moss. The sunlight, except when straight overhead, came through with a dappled pattern on everything. Deer, bear, and an occasional bobcat watched them from the river banks. Birds were everywhere and red-headed woodpeckers chirped out warnings as the party passed them. Owls hooted at them even though it was daylight.

The children were captivated by the colorful Carolina parakeet. Little Henrietta, now five years old, was enthralled by the trip and remembered it for the rest of her life, telling her children and grandchildren about it many times.

The river wandered back and forth for miles. At one point Jean estimated that they had traveled twenty river miles, but were only four miles nearer to their destination. The windings of the river was so extreme that at one point he was surprised when he looked over at the river bank and ten yards further, on the other side of the river bank, he could see the same stretch of river that they were on an hour earlier.

On the fifth day the two young pole men beached the boat upon the bank of the river on the so called, high ground. Jean looked at the land and saw that the high ground might be four or five feet higher than what they had seen all along the trip. He worried about flooding but there was a clearing where they could build shelter until they scouted the area for anything better.

It would be easy to live off the land. There was deer, bear, rabbits, squirrels and numerous other small animals to live off of. There was so many fish in the river that Jean felt they could live off of them forever. They would occasionally need some occasional flour and seasonings from the outside.

The men from Georgetown helped Jean and the others unload the boat and then Jean paid them.

One of the young men said, "Let me tell you about your surroundings. About two or three hours upstream is Lake Waccamaw. There is great fishing there with many varieties that you don't have here in the river. Also, there is a small settlement at the lake where you can get some basic food supplies and gunpowder. If you need anything more you will have to go to Marsh Castle; some people call it White's Plantation. It's a larger settlement and it's about ten miles west of the lake settlement. For anything else you'll have to journey to Wilmington."

"Any people around here?" Jean asked.

"Yes, you will find people scattered throughout your land, mostly ship-wrecked Portuguese survivors who have been here a hundred years and other people who are running from something or just like their privacy." he said.

"Any Indians?"

"No, not really. They have not been around here for fifty or sixty years. Another Indian tribe killed most of them. Oh, yes, I just remembered there is a small settlement of Indians north of the lake about ten or fifteen miles but they are nothing to worry about. They have started farming and they don't bother anyone. Oh, and one last thing, you had better think about what you are going to do if a hurricane hits this area. Build your houses for high water. The winds this far inland will blow down trees but it will not be near what they will have on the coast,"

"Well, thank you for the advice and a good trip. May you have a safe journey home. One last favor though."

"What is that?" they asked.

"If anyone comes, asking questions or looking for us, especially a Frenchman, please tell them nothing," Jean requested, giving them an extra gold coin each.

They smiled and said in their American slang, "Not to worry." They shoved off in their small canoe, waved, and then were gone around a bend of the river.

In Saint-Domingue, Napoleon had sent General Leclerc with an army of 25,000 men to subdue Toussaint. Toussaint played a masterful game of guerilla warfare. He decided to keep his men hidden, strike periodically and wait for the yellow fever to do its job. The strategy worked well. Soon Leclerc had lost half his men to yellow fever and those left could barely function. In a letter to Napoleon, Lecleerc stated that he barely had 200 men who were fit for duty, although this was probably an exaggeration.

Leclerc changed his strategy to subterfuge. He tried and was successful in getting Toussaint's generals to defect to his side with promises of rank and money; even Moyse and Dessaline defected.

With evidence of betrayal by many of his generals and believing that Napoleon would send another army, Toussaint negotiated with Leclerc and was allowed to retire to the Desfauneaux Plantation. Most historians believe he was letting time and the yellow fever do the work for him until a more favorable time for him to reassemble his army.

During this lull, Toussaint was tricked into visiting a neighboring French general's headquarters without a guard escort. This was a general whom he trusted. As he visited, the general excused himself and left the room. Soon soldiers filled the room and arrested Toussaint. He was bound and put on a ship to France where he was soon imprisoned in the cold and damp French prison of Fort de Joux near the French-Swiss border.

Crusoe Island

After the two men left in their small canoe for Georgetown, Jean had all the families gather and they knelt on the ground in prayer.

Jean prayed, *"Dear Lord Jesus, we ask for your protection and guidance as we endeavor to start a new life on this savage but bountiful land. Protect us from the elements and the one who pursues us and keep us from being sent back to certain death in France. Protect our health and help us to have long lives and be prosperous.*

"Forgive us of our past wants to become wealthy at the expense of our fellowman." Jules interjected an amen here. *"All that we ask for now is to be safe and have good health. We ask these blessing in your son, Jesus Christ's holy name. Amen."*

Jean made the sign of the cross, and stood; everyone followed suit. Jean spoke again, "I know that we all miss our home in Saint-Domingue but it became too dangerous for all of us. Now, we must do our best to make this our new home.

After three weeks of hard labor signs of a small settlement began to appear. Everyone helped except for the two smaller children. Jean Gerome, the oldest boy, now five years old, helped by doing small errands. Jeanne could not help. She was weak and exhausted. Belle spent most of her time taking care of Jeanne and the other children.

Three weeks of labor was now showing results. They had built two crude small houses in the American log cabin style. Both had fireplaces with chimneys constructed after a well-identifiable French style. There was one house for the white families and one for Jules' family. In three or four weeks they would have a house for each family.

They had taken the precaution of not building on the ground but on a platform with piers, a couple of feet above the ground in case of flooding. Jules' next project was to disassemble the boat and use the material to build a smaller one, one more suitable for a slow moving and sometime shallow river.

Jules knew how to make furniture and that was his project. The children's job was to catch fish and help where they could.

In Wilmington it had taken Sartre about three weeks to find out that the Formy-Duvals had indeed been there. Bando had gotten the information from some blacks in the area near the De Rossett's plantation. Sartre managed to find out from the Smithville boat captain that a man fitting Dr. Formy-Duval's description, along with some other families, had gone to Smithville.

In Smithville it was easy to find where they had gone. It was a small town and they knew everyone's business. They remembered the families that stayed there for two or three days and then caught a ship to Georgetown.

Georgetown turned out to be a little more difficult. It took him and Bando two more weeks before they found the information they needed. Some dock workers remembered that a couple of young men had taken some families up the Waccamaw River in a fishing boat to land they had bought south of Lake Waccamaw.

Here, Sartre decided that this was a good time for he and Bando to part ways. Bando knew too much about Sartre's mission. Bando knew who sent him, why, and what he planned to do. He did not want Bando to be a witness to his final murderous actions. If needed, he would find some shady individuals here in Georgetown. He would pick men who knew how to keep their mouths shut and whom the authorities would have trouble believing.

Sartre felt he had to buy Bando's silence, so Sartre gave Bando his freedom. A letter made it legitimate. Bando was stunned. Freedom was wonderful but his real objective was to find Zoé. He did not have any money to buy a boat and go up the Waccamaw River so the only thing he could think of was to go back to Wilmington. There he would try the overland trip through Elizabeth town, and the old Indian trail to Lake Waccamaw. From there he would have to make it down the Waccamaw River by what every way he could.

He had no trouble signing on with a merchant ship going to Wilmington as a deck hand, and was back in Wilmington in two days with some wages in his pocket.

He provisioned himself with supplies that some slaves gave him. For protection, he also stole a large butcher knife from a shed on one of the plantations.

He asked directions and started to find Zoé. He estimated it would take him about a week to get to Lake Waccamaw and then another couple of days to work his way down the river and find Zoé. But first he had to get across the Cape Fear River in Wilmington.

It took Bando most of the morning to find someone to give him a ride across the river at Wilmington. It took money to ride the ferry and he had none to spare. Late in the morning he came across another black man with a small boat. Maybe he had come down river from one of those plantations on the river to get some supplies.

"Morning Sir," Bando said, trying to initiate a conversation.

"Morning," he replied and gave a slight tip of his wide brimmed straw hat.

"You going back up river with those supplies," Bando asked in his best broken English.

"Yep, I have to go now, since the tide is beginning to flow up the river," the man said.

Bando noticed that there was an extra paddle in the boat and decided to ask for a ride.

"I need a ride to the other side of the river. I can help you paddle if you will take me to the other side," Bando said.

"Where you headed?'

"Oh, towards Elizabeth town," Bando said but not wanting to say his final destination.

"Get in. I'll take you about five miles upstream where you can find a good place that will put you on the road. I say a road; it's more like a trail, to Elizabeth town,"

"Yes sir, I'll be glad to help you row," Bando said hopping into the boat.

After they had paddled out in the river and moved about five hundred yards upstream, the old black man asked, "Where you from? You don't talk like you're from around here."

This made Bando uneasy. He normally spoke the local Creole dialect in Saint-Domingue with ease and did well with French. The English he was trying to speak now, he had learned while guarding English soldiers back on Saint-Domingue. He knew just enough to get by, but he realized that he could be easily recognized as a foreigner.

Bando saw that the old man was curious. Probably wondering if he was a runaway slave. He needed to satisfy the old man but still be vague as possible.

"I'm just in from the islands. I am a free man and got the papers to prove it," Bando replied.

"Well, don't worry, I don't mean you no harm. I'm familiar with this area. I have been on many a hunting trip with my master and know the area; thought you might needs some help with directions."

Bando was quiet for a few moments and then decided to trust the old man and ask about Lake Waccamaw and the river that flowed out of it.

"I'm thinking about settling in a quiet area where nobody will bother me. I've heard that you can be left alone on the river below Lake Waccamaw," Bando said.

"If the snakes and alligators don't get you!", the old man said with a laugh.

"I can handle them."

The old man chuckled and then became serious. This young man was serious about living in a place where no one could find him. He must be running from something. The old man decided to help.

"Listen, why don't you come with me to the plantation where I live this afternoon?" Bando's face showed alarm. "Don't worry, I'll hide you out in the woods and give you something to eat tonight. Then I'll draw out, in the dirt, how to get to the lake and the river out of it."

Bando thought for a moment and then said, "All right, but I'm not too anxious about getting near a slave plantation."

"Don't worry; I'll get you through the night without being seen. Tomorrow, once you get away from the river and the plantations, the people inland will not pay much attention to you. Don't misunderstand; they will notice you, but because they are poor and don't own slaves...well they just aren't as concerned about it. Ten years ago I could walk all over this area with almost no problem, but since that slave revolt down in the islands and all the killing of white people down there, people here have been a little touchy about blacks wandering around by themselves."

Bando nodded, and kept paddling until they reached a spot near the old man's plantation.

"Get out here and go straight in that direction," the old man said, pointing with his hand. "Find you a place to camp beside a little stream you will find and I'll bring you some food when it starts to get dark. We'll talk about directions for that lake and river."

That evening the old man came like he had promised. He gave Bando some fried pork chops and corn on the cob. Bando had never seen corn before, but he found that it was almost as good as the fried pork chops. It was the best food he had eaten in weeks.

By a small fire the old man drew out maps in the dirt on how to get to Elizabeth town, how to find and follow the old Indian trail to Lake Waccamaw and where the Waccamaw River started its journey south on the southwest side of the lake.

The old man was concerned about one thing though. He said, "You're gonna need a canoe or something to get down the river. Too many snakes to wade it. Sometimes people leave canoes and small boats near the mouth of the river so's they don't have to tote it back and forth to their houses. You might can buy one of those if you have any money. If you don't and decide to take one, just return it as soon as you can. People do that at times and the owners don't get too concerned unless it stays gone too long."

After a while the fire and the conversation died down

and the old man wished Bando luck. They shook hands and the old man left.

The next morning Bando started his walk to Elizabeth town. For breakfast he chewed on one of the corn crackers that the old man had given him. A corn cracker was a type of cornbread that sustained most of the poor whites and blacks. Corn was the main food staple of the poor. The corn crackers were so popular that the well-to-do folks called the common people who ate them *Crackers.*

That afternoon as he was following the trail to Elizabeth town he saw something about forty yards ahead. Bando froze. A bear and her cubs walked out onto the trail. The bear stopped, halfway across the road, and put her nose up in the air. She spotted Bando and stood up on her hind legs.

Instinct told Bando not to turn his back and run. He started walking backwards slowly. He did this for about twenty yards until he backed himself off the road into some brush. He squatted and watched the bear. The bear kept standing for another three or four minutes and then came down and walked into the woods with her cubs.

Bando gave the bear about twenty minutes to clear the area and continued his walk toward Elizabeth town. Late that afternoon, about dusk, he made camp near a stream fifteen yards from the trail. He made a bed from pine straw and leaves and lay down. In a few minutes he heard rustling in the brush. It gave him a scare; he thought maybe another bear was nearby. It turned out to be four turkeys looking for a tree in which to roost. Bando was fascinated by all the wildlife that he was seeing. He thought, *How could anyone go hungry in a land like this?*

The next day was uneventful as far as big game goes, but he saw rabbits, squirrels, raccoons, possums, and a couple of snakes.

That evening he made his usual bed of pine straw and ate his last corn cracker, supplemented by some wild grapes. They were big and sweet. It did not take him long to fall asleep, but he was awakened during the middle of the night by a howling. He couldn't see the panther and didn't know what it was, but it scared the hell out of him. For a few moments Bando thought he saw a pair of red eyes. He built a fire, held a torch in one hand and his butcher knife in the other, and stayed awake the rest of the night.

By the time he reached Elizabeth town the next day he was out of corn crackers, hungry and tired from lack of sleep. Again, friendly blacks smuggled food out of the kitchens for him. There was a difference between this country and Saint-Domingue, a difference between the blacks here and the blacks back home. There was slavery and resentment here for sure, but the animosity between the races was not as strong.

In Saint-Domingue, slaves were usually worked to death within a few years, given barely enough clothing and food to keep them alive. They were a cheap, short-term investment. Here they were still slaves and they were worked hard, but not to death. They were too expensive. There was a friendlier working atmosphere where they tolerated each other. That was not to say that the slaves here were satisfied with the situation; they were not. They did want to be free and live their own lives. The feelings were just was not as intense here as they had been on Saint-Domingue.

The blacks gave him food to take with him and told him how to find the Indian trail to Lake Waccamaw. They told him that he should be able to ask directions or for food at any house, even of whites. They said some would do nothing for you, but some would help. They were right. Many looked at him like he was a leper, some, grudgingly, gave him small amounts of food and some were generous with their food, water, and directions.

The last house he stopped at was a free black family named Graham. They said he was about four miles from the lake. They gave him fresh water and an animal-skin flask so that he could carry some with him. They invited him to stay the rest of the day and spend the night, but he refused. It was only noon and he could reach the lake before dusk. He would remember this family.

Late in the afternoon he reached Lake Waccamaw. He sat down on the bank on the high north side of the lake and rested, enjoying the late afternoon breeze. It was one of the most restful places he had ever seen. He moved to a where no one could see him. He took off his clothes and submerged himself in the shallow water of the lake. He was so tired and it felt so good that he almost went to sleep while floating in the shallow water near the shore.

Later he ate some corn crackers the Grahams had given him; it seemed like everyone ate corn crackers here. As he gazed across the lake, he tried to guess the location of the river mouth. He was going to try to limit his contact with people until he found Zoé and do whatever he had to do to take her with him. He would find the mouth of the river tomorrow.

The next day Bando found the mouth of the river in the late afternoon and a canoe tied to a tree branch about twenty yards downstream. He left a coin stuck in the tree where he found the canoe. He decided to spend the night there. He would rather not start now with only two hours of daylight left and fumble around in the dark to make a camp.

Jules was making furniture on his new workbench. It had taken him two or three days to build it, and the jigs so he could begin to make furniture. He was finishing a chair for Madam Jeanne. He knew how to make chairs but he had seen this one in Georgetown. He had never seen one like it, it had rockers on the bottom of the chair, and naturally the Americans called it a rocking chair.

It took him a while to figure out the proper leg angles and how to fit them into the rockers but after several attempts he did it. He sat the rocker on the ground and tried it.

Madam Jean ought to like this, he thought. Everyone was worried about her; she was very sick.

Jean had unpacked one of the large chests filled with medical instruments. Jean was spending much of his time trying to find trees, bushes, and vines that he was familiar with to make medicine for Jeanne. He gathered some leaves of various trees and took out his large lignum vitae mortar bowl and pestle. He also took out a small set of scales to weigh medicines and began to mix some medicine to be brewed for Jeanne to drink.

Jules took the rocking chair and placed it on the crude porch of the house.

"Belle," he called out softly so as not to disturb Jeanne.

Belle came out and said, "What do you have there, Jules?"

"It's a rocking chair. I thought Madam Jeanne might enjoy sitting outside for a spell and rocking in the sun," Jules said.

"You sure that it's safe? It won't throw her out, will it?" Belle asked.

"No, no, this is what all the Americans use. Everyone has a rocking chair," Jules said

"All right, then. Help me get her out of the bed and out here," Belle said.

Belle went inside and asked Jeanne, "Madam Jeanne, don't you want to sit in Jules' new chair out on the porch. He put rockers on it."

"Yes, I think I would like to sit in the sunshine and see if that would make me feel any better,"

They lifted Jeanne out of bed and helped her into the chair.

It took Jeanne a few moments to catch her breath and gather the strength to start the rocking motion with her feet.

The sun felt good on her face and she said, "Oh, I like this chair, Jules. It's so comfortable. I believe I could take a nap right here, just rocking in the sun."

Belle and Jules smiled at each other and Belle left to see what the younger children were doing. Jules returned to his work bench to start another piece of furniture. He could still keep an eye on Jeanne who was slowly rocking on the porch.

That evening at supper they tried to get Jeanne to eat but she barely ate anything.

"Jeanne, please drink this medicine I made for you. I think it will make you feel better," Jean said.

"I'll try. Everything seems to upset my stomach."

Jean was able to get her to drink most of the medicinal brew. It made her drowsy and she was soon asleep.

Jean looked around their little settlement. They had made a great deal of progress. They had all learned from Jules. Under his direction all the men had learned enough carpentry to build cabins, sheds, a small pier on the river and numerous other little items. The De Rossset and Cluveires families were building their own cabins. Jean built his own medicinal shed where he mixed plants for medicine.

All this was not easy. For each project they had to cut trees, strip, and split them, and only then were they able to use it to build a cabin or piece of furniture.

Yesterday, two men from the area had pulled up to their pier to see who they were. They spoke English and said their family had been in this area for two or three generations. He said his father, a Ben Crusoe, now dead, had come here about sixty years ago. The men showed Jean's group some building tricks, some fishing techniques, and numerous other helpful hints for living in the swamp.

It was dusk and Jean realized there was a quiet beauty here in his swamp: the trees with their Spanish moss, the numerous ferns that spread throughout the swamp, and the wildlife that lived in it.

He thought if they could live here in peace for a couple of years and get over the trauma of the past ten to twelve years of war and running for their lives then maybe they could have a normal life and raise their children without worry.

It was time to turn in and get some rest for tomorrow.

Blood on the River

"How far are we from the lake?" Sartre asked his guide.

"About a half day."

Sartre found a guide, suitably shady enough, to take him up the river to find Dr. Formy-Duval. He bought a pair of flintlock pistols and took some practice shots during the first part of the voyage to make sure he knew what he was doing and could hit a target a short distance away.

They had been on the river for three and a half days. If they were a half day from the lake then they should be coming upon the high ground soon. This had to be where they would be settling.

"Be quiet. We may be getting near them. I don't want to let them know that we're here." About that time he heard children's laughter around the next bend in the river.

"Shhhh," Sartre said. He pointed a finger to the right bank, indicating to his guide where he wanted to land the boat. They pulled the small boat on shore, pulled their flintlock pistols, and squatted quietly, listening. After five minutes they started making their way through the brush toward the sounds. Sartre was hoping that there was no dog to warn them.

Sartre and his guide crept through the swamp until they came upon the edge of the settlement. They stayed there for about twenty minutes, watching to see where everyone was and especially for Dr. Formy-Duval.

Had Jean and Jules been in the swamp for a few more months and learned the sounds of nature, they would have realized the absence of the birds singing and the chatter of squirrels making a loud fuss was a warning.

It was noon and most of the people in the clearing were going to one of the houses for lunch. A lady sitting in a rocking chair on a front porch appeared to be asleep. He had seen what he thought was everyone except for the doctor. Then he saw him. On the far side of the clearing was a small shed where he saw a man working. He was almost certain it was Dr. Formy-Duval.

Sartre told his guide, "Take this gun and corner everyone in the house and make them lie on the floor. I'll go after the doctor. If no one sees me kill the doctor then we may not have to kill anyone else, but if they do, then we will have to kill them all."

Sartre gave the signal to his guide for them to move in.

Inside the house, Belle asked Zoé, "Cher, go out back and get another bucket of water out of the water barrel."

They had rigged a fresh water collection system with the rain water coming off the roof into some homemade gutters and into a barrel.

"Yes, mamma." Zoé was coming around the corner of the house with the water when she saw two men running her way with guns. She screamed and ran toward the shed where Dr. Formy-Duval was working.

Her scream alerted everyone in the house and the doctor in the shed. He stepped outside and saw Zoé running toward him with Sartre in pursuit.

"Come with me!" Jean said and grabbed Zoé's hand. They ran into the swamp. After ten yards Jean said, "Zoé hide in those bushes beside the river." Jean ran on, noisily at first, to pull Sartre away from Zoé.

Sartre could see Jean running about thirty feet ahead of him. He stopped, aimed, and fired.

The shot grazed Jean's arm but with all the excitement Jean never felt it. He finally reached a thick brush line and disappeared into it. Sartre followed. It became a game of cat and mouse. Jean was trying to work his way along the back of the clearing to get to the house, his family and friends.

Sartre reloaded and decided that he would try to find the girl he saw running with the doctor and use her as bait to get the doctor to come out. He started backtracking to where they first entered the clearing and retraced his footsteps for about ten yards in the swamp to the place where he fired at the doctor.

He stopped and looked around carefully. He started following the brush line beside the river. Then he saw something. It was a small piece of white linen showing though some bushes.

He made his way toward the bush but looked in the other direction away from the bush. When he reached the bush he suddenly reached down and pulled it aside.

Zoé screamed as Sartre grabbed her by the arm and pulled her up.

"Well, what a pretty little thing we have here. I might have some fun with you before I slit your pretty little throat,"

He spun Zoé around to where he had her back up against his body. One hand held her there and one hand held his gun.

Zoé screamed again.

Sartre felt an arm come around his neck and a stabbing pain in his back. He thought, *How did the doctor manage to do this to me?* The last thing he saw as he fell into the river was Bando standing there with a large butcher knife. Blood mixed with the dark tannic stains of the river.

Zoé flung both arms around Bando and sobbed, "You came for me. You came for me."

"Come on, we have to get out of here. I have a canoe." Bando said.

"No!" Zoé said. "We have to save the rest. There is another man who is going to kill the others. My mother is there."

Bando took a deep breath. He thought he was through here, but if Zoé was to go with him, he had to help save the others.

Bando and Zoé walked into the clearing and toward the house. The guide saw them coming. He had forced the others on the floor inside the house, but left the sick old lady in her rocker on the front porch. She presented no danger and he had other things to do.

As Bando and Zoé came near the guide Jean walked out of the woods on the other side. All three walked towards him.

The guide looked at them and snarled, "You think you have me surrounded, don't ye. Well, I have the gun, so who's going to be brave enough to be first. And after that I have a nice big ole knife for the rest of you."

Then he noticed Bando's butcher knife and the blood on it. He knew Sartre must be dead. He pointed his pistol at Bando and said, "Well, I guess you should be first."

Bando stopped, but Zoé continued toward the house and stopped about two or three paces from the front step, about five feet from the guide.

The guide pointed his pistol at the doctor, then at Zoé and finally at Bando and said, with a crazed laugh, "Goodbye."

At that moment Zoé pulled Sartre's gun out from a fold in her skirt, pointed it at the guide's chest and pulled the trigger. "Goodbye," Zoé said cheerfully.

The guide staggered a second with a stunned look of "How the hell did that happen?" and fell to the ground.

Dr. Jean walked over and knelt to examine the guide to see if he was dead. He was.

Everyone came out of the house and into the yard.

Belle came out the door and saw Zoé with her arms around Bando and smiled. Her little girl had finally got her man. Then she noticed Jeanne.

Something was wrong with Jeanne's stare. She walked over to the rocking chair. She was dead. Belle let out a moan and then a sob.

Jean looked up and saw Belle crying with Jeanne's head cradled against her breast. He knew.

Jean rushed to the porch and knelt next to Jeanne and took her head and put it on his shoulder.

Jean whispered in Jeanne's ear, "It's over now, Princess. You don't have to suffer anymore, no more pain, no more of those horrible nightmares and no more terrible things to run from." He choked slightly and then finished, "Go find little Louis and wait for me."

Epilogue

Jeanne was buried two miles north of Lake Waccamaw in a field beside a lone cedar tree. This was done so there would never be flooding to disturb her. Jean eventually bought this field and land for his farming enterprises. Using a neighbor's apple cider press he baled the first bale of cotton in that county.

Jean remarried and had more children. There are Formy-Duvals all over southeastern North Carolina and the state of North Carolina. Many have shortened their name to Duval, but many, proud of their heritage, kept the original spelling.

Jean's son, Jean Gerome, followed in his father's footsteps and became a successful farmer and served in the War of 1812.

His daughter, Henrietta, married and settled down in Fayetteville, North Carolina.

The youngest son, Alexander, became a lawyer and was elected as a state representative to the North Carolina Legislature from 1825-1826. He left soon after his first term and moved to north Florida and also served in the Florida Territorial Legislature from 1839-1841.

There are several artifacts of Dr. Formy-Duval's on display at the Depot Museum in Lake Waccamaw, North Carolina. Featured are some of Dr. Formy-Duval's medical instruments. They include his large wooden lignum vitae mortar bowl, a small metal mortar and pestle, and a small set of scales used to weigh out medicines. There is also a portrait of Dr. Formy-Duval that was enlarged and painted from a knee buckle cameo.

Descendants of Dr. Formy-Duval took the French land deeds and financial documents that proved the doctor's ownership of lands in Saint-Domingue and France to a law firm in Wilmington in the late 1800s. This was an effort to claim reparations from the French government for lost lands during the Haitian Slave Revolt. The claim was assigned to a young lawyer who was new to the firm. Within a week the lawyer disappeared along with all the Formy-Duval land deeds and documents, much to the despair of the Formy-Duvals and the embarrassment of law firm.

Bando and Zoé settled down on a small farm beside the Grahams, the only other free black family in the area. They had several children and two of them married some of the Graham children. Because of their French and Saint-Domingue heritage, their children talked differently than the other blacks. They spoke English but they had a high-pitch chatter and cadence that was heavily influenced by their French-Caribbean roots and their grandparents, Belle and Jules, who later joined Zoé and Bando on their small farm.

The De Rossetts and the Cluveires stayed in the Crusoe Island area. Their names slowly became more Americanized, finally becoming Ross and Clewis. Crousilleau Island became known as Crusoe Island. The people who stayed on and around Crusoe Island continued to be isolated and reclusive for the next 120 years.

Most outsiders did not want to associate with the *swamp people*. Law officers who ventured into Crusoe rarely came out, and the Crusoe people still went crazy over the sight of a black person until the early 1900s. To this day many black people in the area are wary about entering Crusoe. This atmosphere of fear began to wane when Kinchen Council began his friendship with Buck Clewis in the early 1900s. Mr. Council's influence as a county commissioner started the process of bringing Crusoe into the Twentieth Century by providing roads, schools and home demonstration agents.

Signs of the old way of life and architecture still existed until the 1940s, but if you drive into Crusoe today you will not be able to distinguish the road and houses from any other country road in North Carolina; although a few of the old timers still have that distinctive halting dialect in their speech; almost a musical way of talking.

In Europe, Toussaint was no match for the cold French prison on the Swiss border. Napoleon made certain that Toussaint's prison life was miserable and sure to bring a slow torturous death. He had his food and drink cut to starvation levels. Toussaint shivered constantly because Napoleon gave orders that he was not to be provided enough firewood for his cell. It was cold and wet and frost formed on walls each night. Mental isolation was also strictly enforced. There was absolutely no contact with anyone outside of the cell. The final blow came when the commandant of the jail went on a four-day journey. He ordered no contact or provisions for Toussaint and took the key to his cell with him. When he returned he found Toussaint dead in a chair beside a burned-out fire.

He was buried within the walls of the prison. Years later they remodeled the prison and dug up all the prison graves and tossed the remains down a cliff. There is no visible grave or bones left to memorialize this remarkable man.

The United States owes a great deal to Toussaint. He helped divert Napoleon's plans to invade the southern

United States and wore down his army, so that Napoleon eventually gave up on the invasion and an attempt for a North American empire.

In fact, a couple of years later, when Thomas Jefferson sent envoys to Paris to inquire about purchasing New Orleans, Napoleon countered with a different offer. He felt that the whole Louisiana Territory was lost and it was only a matter of time before the English would sweep down from Canada and take it. To keep England from getting the territory, and much to the surprise of the American envoys, he offered them the whole Louisiana Territory for a mere 15 million dollars.

The United States borrowed the money from English banks, paid France for the territory, and Napoleon used the money to finance his war against England.

The acquisition of the Louisiana Territory by the United States was a great irritant to England. Wanting to hold back America's growth, they tried to reverse the acquisition during the *War of 1812* at the *Battle of New Orleans.* The English hoped to gain control of both the Mississippi River and the Louisiana Territory, but they were soundly defeated at the Chalmette battlefield by General Andrew Jackson's army.

Jefferson's purchase of the Louisiana Territory set the stage for the sometimes, now maligned, *Manifest Destiny*, all because a 50-plus year old black man in Saint-Domingue (Haiti) fought off three European armies, stopped Napoleon's conquest of the southern United States, and established the first Black government in the Western Hemisphere.

Haiti could have been an important nation in the Caribbean but Toussaint's deceitful and greedy generals betrayed him and his ideals. They took the island back to traditional slavery. The generals had their own plantations run with slaves whom they treated no better than the white planters had. They also dealt in slave trading.

Had Napoleon's French Directorate not deceived Toussaint and had he been allowed to establish a government he envisioned, a nation built on freedom and trade with other nations, then Haiti would probably be a much different nation today. Toussaint's succeeding generals, not being able to grasp his vision and combined with their unbridled greed, led Haiti into the miserable fortune it has today.

...Though fallen thyself, never to rise again,
Live, and take comfort. Thou hast left behind
Powers that will work for thee; air, earth and skies;
There's not a breathing of the common wind
That will forget thee;...

<u>Toussaint L'Ouverture</u> *From A Sonnet By William Wordsworth*

The End

Centaur of the Savannahs

Bibliography

Citizen Toussaint, by Ralph Korngold, Little, Brown and Co., Boston, 1945

The Haitian Revolution 1789-1804 – Thomas O. Ott, The University of Tennessee Press, 1973

Letters of Toussaint Louverture and of Edward Stevens, 1798-1800, The American Historical Review, Volume XVI, October 1910 to 1911, Pages 64-101.

Jefferson and the Leclerc Expedition, The American Historical Review, Volume XXXIII, October 1927 to July 1928, Pages 322-328.

Chalmette: The Battle of New Orleans and How the British Nearly Stole the Louisiana Territory – Charles Patton, Hickory Tales Publishing, Bowling Green, Ky., April 2001.

About Charles Patton

After Charles Patton graduated from the University of Middle Tennessee he served as a Naval Officer and Pilot for several years, following which he worked as an Engineer and Plant Manager and presently works in local government.

Charles has previously written a history of the Battle of New Orleans, called *Chalmette*, published by the Hickory Tales Publishing Co. and a novel, *Crousilleau*, which won the Clark Cox Historical Fiction Award in 2010, and *Oriental Flyer* published by Second Wind Publishing 2013. Charles, his wife Sylvia, and Velcro the cat live at Lake Waccamaw, NC.